TO RECEIVE
MY SERVICES
YOU MUST BE
DYING AND ALONE

I0716018

To Receive My Services
You Must Be Dying And Alone

STORIES BY **KATHRYN KRUSE**

JACKLEG PRESS

JackLeg Press
jacklegpress.org

www.kathrynkruse.com

ISBN: 978-1956907124

Library of Congress Control Number: 2023945616

Cover art: Ashley Siebels

PRAISE FOR KATHRYN KRUSE

The stories in Kathryn Kruse's collection startle with their attention to our most elemental selves: our bodies, our work, our health, our language. We share these traits with the characters, and what's startling is not so much the familiar moments, as the ways in which moments both familiar and unfamiliar intersect and entangle themselves into unusual arrangements. There are the insistent e-mails in one story promising money, power, and love, and the ways in which they seem addressed to one particular person, with one particular name, until they replicate and multiply. It could be anyone, you think. It could be you. There are familiar corporate vistas and workshops and culture, all of them turned strange and beautiful as we run through the possibilities of living here, right now, in late capitalism—the injuries and victories of "Fun Land," for example, or the narrator of the title story, who asks that you be dying and alone. The stories suggest that one of these requirements is true and inevitable, the other maybe less so. We're never fully alone, this extraordinary collection suggests. Someone's always trying to reach us. These stories are a wonderful reminders of that truth—shockingly accurate, bracingly funny, wonderful company all around.

—Juan Martinez, author of *Extended Stay*

The stories in *To Receive My Services You Must Be Dying and Alone* are as compelling as I've read in recent memory. Driven by compassion, fueled by a passionate intelligence, Kathryn Kruse's fictions make the reader pause and consider the depths of their humanity. There is much humor and pathos in *To Receive My Services*. Above all, there is grace and beauty. Read this book and be changed by it.

—Pablo Medina, author of *The Cuban Comedy*

Kathryn Kruse's new collection of stories is dizzying and provocative. Through razor sharp writing, she depicts a world in which grief leads a man to taxidermy his late wife and where a minstrel finds love with a series of literal logs. But intimacy is the soul and subject here, and it manifests in surprising, revealing ways, such as a tender imaginary backrub between videochat lovers. Throughout, she never takes her foot off the gas, and, even at their darkest, every story, like the ride in "Fun Land," which features a misanthropic nurse on duty for a theme-park catastrophe, is a dervish of fun!

—Jeff Parker, author of *Ovenman*

TABLE OF CONTENTS

Thanks, RSK

TO RECEIVE MY SERVICES
YOU MUST BE DYING AND ALONE

Lots of people ask to be held. When it comes right down to it they are about to go tits up and it doesn't matter who the hell I am, that we've never met before. They cling to my warm and living body and I am comfort. I am their sister and brother, teacher, first girlfriend and their last lover. Fifteen-year-old girls turn and say, *Please make love to me. I don't want to die without knowing.* Seventy-year-old men lose their gruff and say, *My wife, she didn't touch me for the past five years. Let's close our eyes and hold hands.*

Sometimes I sit in a chair. Sometimes I lie in the bed. I put cool hands on cheeks, on collar bones. I twine my fingers with theirs. I ease the dying. I calm. Others say I love.

My name is Sally. It's a crap sort of name. Most people forget it the moment it's out of my mouth, while I'm still introducing myself. A lot of old people have the best names. Bertram and Eudaleia. I'd probably name my kids something wonderful like that, call them Bertie and Lea if they liked, but I don't suppose I'll have kids. It's funny, I talk to nurses who say every time they see someone cash in, the first thing they want is to head home and reproduce, dig their fingers deep into the physical beauty of life. Not me. Think about those nuns out on battlefields. Sure they probably had a profound connection with their God, married to the cross or whatever, but I bet if you pushed hard enough a few would admit that the real flesh and fragile bones of children weren't in the cards after seeing what happens to all that flesh, how easily bone shatters. Me too. But I'm not joining any convents.

I'm not quite sure how Frank got in, how, after days, I still found his voice messages waiting each time I left ICUs and hospice cares.

Frank, he missed his wife's death. It was blood clots. Rachel was young, thirty-four, no family history, no medical problems and the thing went fast while Frank was out of town at a conference. He deals in Tupperware.

I was finishing up with a car accident when a nurse I'd worked with a few times tapped my shoulder and asked if I'd come. *Just got a feeling on this one*, she said. *Clotting and internal bleeding at the same time. That's never good.*

Frank arrived ten minutes after Rachel's death. A while later he found me in the cafeteria drinking coffee. His complexion seemed waxy and he'd lost his sports jacket somewhere, exposing a rumpled shirt. He ran his hands down the sides of his pudgy midriff searching for pockets that were not there, but otherwise he didn't seem too bad. I didn't think he'd be a wailer or throw anything.

"I've done it. All the paperwork," he said.

"Yes. There is lots of that," I said.

Then we were silent. Frank gave up on finding the pockets and fidgeted with a scrap of paper he picked up from the table. His hair seemed longer, shaggier, than I'd expected for a salesman. I sighed. I started to ask if he wanted a coffee and he said, "We're new to the city. Only a few days. No family or anything."

He felt embarrassed, I think.

"Plenty of people die when no one can be with them. It's a part of our lifestyle." I have found this statement calms people.

"How...?" he asked.

"Peaceful. She held my hand. She said your name. She had no pain."

"Oh. Thank you."

"Thanks," he said again. He looked back and forth from ceiling to the paper shreds in his fingers. I thought he'd ask for details about his wife's death. I hoped he wouldn't. I felt tired, two cases in a row, and Rachel had been a confessor and I didn't want to have to make decisions about true and honest.

"Do you know good places to deal with. To preserve her?" he asked.

"Oh. Like a funeral parlor?"

"Well, I suppose. Or. Anything else?" He gave me a sideways glance that I couldn't read. Frank had a wide face and large, thick glasses that often caught reflections and made his eyes look lopsided and stretched, his expressions difficult to read.

"Sorry," I said. "I don't do much with arrangements after the death."

"I just thought, because of, you know, your job, you might know." He held his breath, trapping the rest of what he wanted to say in his lungs.

We sat for a bit longer and then Frank left to go home.

I have several form letters that I send to people after the checks have cleared. They start with something like, *To the bereaved of _______, I wish to express my deepest condolences at your loss. Having spent a small amount of time with your _______ I can understand any sorrow you feel at his/her/their departure from your life/lives. As I had the honor of being with _______ during his/her/their final moments I thought it might relieve your mind/minds to know that he/she/they died* and then there are several options: *peacefully./with your name on his/her/their lips./with great bravery./after a certain amount of distress that made the quiet and calm of final rest a great relief.* And so on. Of course, if people ask for details I'll tell them how their loved ones were so doped they couldn't have felt pain if the nurses took a cattle prod to them, or that there was screaming and fecal matter, or that we sang songs, that their eyelids flickered a few times but they never gained any real consciousness, that their bodies shook, that they held my hand hard, so I still have the bruises, and, as their grip loosened, I thought of paper boats floating out to sea.

Interestingly, most people don't ask. I'm always shocked by that, but generally the form letter, a sketch of the last moments, a picture that they can fill in on their own or leave empty is all they want.

A few days later I got my first call from Frank. I was with Marjorie, an old woman who had decided to die and called me every time she thought the moment might be upon her. She and her husband, George, lived in a nursing home. He'd suffered a hemorrhagic stroke that pushed him into a coma. The day he moved from the ICU into the hospice section of their nursing home Marjorie began to refuse food. She still lived down in their old suite, but the staff put a small cot in George's room, and she spent most of her days there with him. I had been called in a few times, each visit her fingers more frail when she gripped my hands. I sat at her bedside, and we talked about books. I played Puccini. I don't know what the correlation is, but lots of people who die alone want to listen to opera in their final hours. Maybe people like to think the full orchestra plays for them, crescendos at their last breath, audience in tears. During pauses in the music and the conversation we heard George's shallow breath rustle over on his side of the room.

Eventually, each time I came, Marjorie started fidgeting with the sheets drawn up around her and looked over at husband's slack face, sat up and said, "Well, honey, I think I was wrong. Soon I'll be moving along to the next place with George. But I guess it's not my time quite yet."

When my phone rang I started to apologize for forgetting to turn it off. Marjorie said, "No, no. Go ahead and answer it. Is it a gentleman?" She winked at me. I expected Frank to be calling with a funeral invite, but he asked if I wouldn't stop by for coffee.

"I hope you can come. You see, like I said, we just moved here. I hardly know anyone. It's hard to start conversations. 'Hi. My wife just died. I'd like to be friends.'"

I could see Marjorie looking at George and her chest rose and fell with his breath while Calaf sang "Nessun dorma".

I agreed to coffee and cursed myself when I hung up the phone.

Marjorie did not die that day.

On my business card it says *Consultant* and *to receive my services you must be dying and alone.* I am self-employed, charge an hourly rate and accept my own clients.

I do not do the still living. What I mean is I don't get mixed up in the friends and the relatives of those that I've helped to pass on.

I know plenty of cultures have mourners, paid professionals, who come to the sides of graves and pyres and tear their hair and rend their clothing. That's not me. You show up for a terminal illness, for bleeds into the brain and stage IV cancer and you know that a light, so to speak, gleams at the end. A conclusion to the relationship. Get taken in by the family, let the wife smudge her mascara all over you, drink scotch with the son, and that's it, *Uncle Leroy move on down a spot. Put the extra leaf in the table. I'll be seeing you at Christmas and all the birthdays.*

The families of those who die with me, they couldn't imagine forking over cash to strangers performing sorrow. *Insincere,* they'd think. *Asking an outsider to wash our dirtiest undies.* But when they finally get to the hospital, people who rushed but didn't make it in time, most are unsure what to do next. If their knees want to give out and if they'd like to slam their hands on the ground till the gray linoleum shines bloody with their grief, they hold themselves back, their family members tsk and whisper, *Roger, Beth, let's keep it together, now.* If they can't quite cry at that moment, they worry they have done something wrong. I see these people, unprepared for death, look at me out of the corners of their eyes, like someone at a dinner party trying to figure out what fork to use with the salad, begging me, a little, to teach them how to demonstrate grief. All the time they ask me to *just say a few words at the funeral.* Anything I could say would be inauthentic, a representation, a remolding of the truth, and I don't do inauthentic. I don't do funerals because funerals are for the still living.

Frank lived in a small, rented one-flat. The front door opened into a living room that had poor lighting and dark carpeting covered in stacks of still unopened moving boxes.

"Come into the kitchen," he said.

The coffee maker sat on top of a column of boxes, the cardboard under the machine stained from water he'd spilled filling the back chamber. Two chairs hovered in the middle of the linoleum and the table leaned in several unassembled pieces against a wall. Amid the disorder, besides a few cooking utensils sprouting from a ceramic vase, the counters gleamed bare.

"Rachel, you know, she was looking for a job. Floral design. I sell reusable plastic food storage devices."

"Oh," I said. "Tupperware?"

"I can't call it that. Here." He pulled a box up off the ground. As he handed it to me the ceiling lights reflected off his glasses.

"Sit. Sit," he said.

Inside the box was a large set of rectangular food-storage devices, laid one inside the other like simple Russian dolls.

"An extra thank you, because." He waved his hand in the air and let it come to rest, for a moment, on the hairline above his temple.

I said, "You don't have to."

"Well."

"Thank you."

"Yes," he said, clapping his hands. He sloshed coffee into two cups, handed one to me and then sat down in the other chair. They were arranged so that we both faced the stove.

We took sips of coffee.

"Come on," Frank said. "I want to show you something."

He led me back to the living room. Our feet stirred a musty smell into the air.

"Maybe sit," he pointed to an overstuffed couch, the brown upholstery pilling and rough, piled with clothes and books. Even in the darkness I could tell that the clothes were Rachel's.

Frank said, "No, no. That's ok. Just stand."

He flipped a switch and a row of cheap track lighting screwed in over the opposite corner came on.

In the shadow of an empty bookcase stood Rachel. Frank grabbed my wrist and pulled me towards her. "Sally, here is Rachel."

"Frank," I said, weaker than I'd have liked.

"I've had her stuffed," he said. "Nicely done, isn't it? Died on Thursday and got her back this morning. Monday. Exactly how I asked. Reasonable pricing. Left hand on hip, the other hand balling up her skirt like that. I toyed with the idea of having her posed with her arms up, her fingers clawed, like roaring, like with her mouth like this, you know. I'd say, 'That's how she died!' But I figured the joke would get old. And, well, like you said, that's not how she died."

I got out of there fast. *Thanks for the coffee and I've got a client out at St. Ruth's.* On the street I took great gulps of air and sunshine.

Let me be clear, it wasn't the taxidermy bit that got me out of Frank's place. Whatever. No skin off my elbows if you want to stuff your wife. That's certainly not the strangest thing I've ever heard. People want to be plastered into the walls of houses, shot out of cannons. There are entire civilizations that eat their dead or dismember them to scatter limbs to different winds and deities. Anyone who wants can have their loved one pressurized into the gem of their choice. *Is that a ruby? No. It's Carl.* Once I had this woman ask me to film her brother's feet after he died. She wanted to capture the final growth, the last push, that millimeter of collagen that rises up after death. So there I was, running up the damn hallway after his gurney, sheet over his face, little piggies exposed, trying to hold the camcorder straight. She wept when I handed over the tape and told me she had set up a screen in her living room and would keep his toes projected there on a looped track. You think I'm joking? Go out in the street. People are weird. Doesn't mean they get any less weird when confronted with the inevitability of a dead body. The house of the soul, if you will.

If Frank didn't care about possible legal ramifications, I didn't care that Frank had found someone willing to gut his wife and saturate her skin with ethanol. Not so far from what your average mortician does, as I understand it. No. It was all her clothes sitting on the couch. The way he hadn't unpacked any of his own things. How he said, "Here is Rachel," as if she might hear him. Frank asked me over to help him pretend that Rachel was undead, that that last breath, the stopping of her kidneys and heart, the relaxing and then stiffening of her fingers, hadn't really happened. I had those fingers curled in mine when it started, that last breath, so I was the only one who could reverse the event for Frank. Break the evil spell and say it ain't so.

That might be a bit much. Frank wanted one other person to pretend that the soul was still in the body. It didn't matter who that person was. As I said, I do death. I don't do the living. And when it is time for the living to be dead, I won't help bring them back. So I got out of there.

Before she went into her brief coma, after she seemed to accept that if anything happened suddenly Frank might not be there, after she made sure I knew she didn't want to linger if her condition was incurable or irreversible, Rachel asked me to climb into the hospital bed. She held my hand and talked. She fell quiet for a moment and then kissed me. Usually I'm good at diverting kisses to the cheek or keeping it to a gentle brushing of the lips, but Rachel held my hip and kissed me hard, the rubber oxygen tube in her nose making noises that reminded me of the wheels on plastic toy trucks.

Frank started to call and, every time, I promised myself I'd delete the voicemails without listening.

Like a moth to a flame, I said each time I pressed the play icon to listen. *Like a damn saint to a leper colony.*

"Sally. Hi. Frank. Um. Rachel's husband. You forgot your Tupperware. I mean your food-storage devices. When you came for coffee. I've got them here. Just. Whenever you want to come for them. OK. Well."

"Sally. Frank. Rachel's husband. I'm here. I wanted to make sure the message went through. So. Yes. OK."

"Hi. Yes. This is Frank. Rachel's husband. I'm here with Rachel. Well. You know. I'm just calling to see how you are. Frank. With the food storage. You know. Listen. Come by whenever. For them. Yes. And there is something. I thought maybe you could help. I think. I was thinking. I kept all of her clothes. Rachel. Rachel's. You know. And change her. Sometimes. That sounds weird. Like a baby. Change her. I think her clothes should change sometimes. I guess you…"

I stopped the message.

"Yes. Hi. Hi. Frank. Hi. There is something I didn't tell you when you were here. About Rachel. The guy who did it, who, um, what's it, preserved. Yes.

Well. In the hospital, after you left. Well. And after they'd taken Rachel. It's so hard, Sally. I got on the plane, when I left to the conference, and I thought about her going back home to unpack. She was going to the flower store and the paper store first. On the way home. Did I tell you that, besides the flower arranging, she does this origami stuff, these folded paper flowers in her bouquets? She did this wreath, once, and wove it with tiny white and pink paper flowers. The first time I saw it was at night. I got home late and there, with only the light coming in from the kitchen, it was lying on the couch. At our old house. Back in. Anyway, the way the light caught it was like, like a little galaxy on the couch, all the white flowers catching the light. But just bent pieces of paper. I still have it. Like a crown. For a goddess. I'd like to believe in goddesses. What was I talking about?" He breathed quietly a while. I put my finger on the phone to erase the message but his voice began again. "Right. It's hard, Sally. She was alive. And then gone. Not just dead. Not her dead body. But they took it away and then she was gone. I wanted to see it. The clot. I told the man, the guy, that I wanted the clot in a jar. That, when he opened her up, I'd make it worth his while to find it, to drop it in some formaldehyde. He couldn't find it. He said that. Couldn't be sure. He didn't want to sell me anything inauthentic. Anyway. I thought you might like to know that."

"Sally. Yes. Just checking in about the bill. This is Frank. Rachel's. You know. I dropped it. The address on your card. I thought. I've been thinking. Maybe something happened to it. The check I didn't hand it to you. Directly. So. Sally. You know how I told you about the blood clot. Well, I've been thinking. A lot. About her organs. You don't, so much, when someone is alive, think about their organs. They said, the doctors, what good health she was in. To comfort me, maybe. I can't help but look at her. There she is in that top. Is that a blouse? I don't even know the right words. I guess she looks comfortable. And I think about her organs. Her perfect, healthy organs. Her intestine. Her spleen. Spleen. They would be plump. And slick. Well. I should go."

"Hi. This was part of it. When I got home, after the hospital, there weren't any flowers or paper. I guess she hadn't gone to the flower store or anything. OK."

Rachel had affairs while Frank left to sell reusable food-storage devices, she told me. One of the things, maybe the only thing, she and Frank had in common was that they'd both lost their parents and had no siblings. They'd been adrift and then bumped against one another. She had been thinking of divorcing him. She said that it was time for their boats to stop bouncing against each other. Since they'd met, Frank had wanted her to climb aboard his boat, let hers bob away. She floated her hands with needles taped into the back sides up above her body, toward the tiled ceiling. The soft inner edges tapped against each other in time with the heart monitor and then one hand fluttered up and away, stretched as far as she could reach, and Rachel folded her hands over her chest and closed her eyes for a while. I don't lie, though. I didn't lie to her husband. Before the brief coma, her eyes went flat and she said, *Frank.*

Marjorie had been ten days without food when she called again. George had not died. When the hospice volunteer showed me into his room, both lay under handmade quilts. Red and yellow stars triangled across their chests and a copy of *La Traviata* I'd lent Marjorie played. George had sunk deeper into his bed and I knew he wouldn't last long. Some people can read the stock market. I can read death. Just takes some practice. Before she told me to go home that day Marjorie beat me at checkers three times. Then she reached up her thin, thin hand and tugged gently at the front of my hair. She said, "Well, I don't know how long I'll have to wait, but I guess I didn't get the call today. I'll kiss George on the cheek and go downstairs for a bit."

The next time he called I answered. "Frank."

"Sally."

"Frank, you have got to stop calling me."

"Yes. I suppose."

"Frank, I provided a service for your wife and now our relationship is over."

"Yes. But you. Your storage devices."

"Thank you. But I'd like you to keep those."

"Sally."

"Frank. You need to get out and do things. You need to call other people."

"Sally."

I knew that I should end the conversation, that I should not engage any further, but there was something so hurt in how he'd said my name, *Sally*, that kept me talking. Most people say my name with very little thought. After a small bit of effort to get the *Sa* out, *lly* sort of dribbles along behind. But Frank had said the whole name, *Sally*, with a sort of music. It reminded me of the death scene in *La bohème* when Rodolfo wails, *Mimi*. I told myself, *Get off the phone. Get off the phone*. But I was still on the phone.

"When was the last time you were out of the house?"

"I don't know. Your check. Taking your check."

"When was the last time you saw anyone?"

"Coffee."

"Your family? Rachel's family?"

"They won't be coming."

I already knew the answer. Rachel had told me. I wanted to make him say it. Ha. I'll Carmen your Mimi.

But then I said, "I'm going to play racquetball tomorrow. You can come if you like."

I did not expect him to have sports goggles. He didn't seem the athletic type. It made me feel better, like when Cyrano kicks those guys' butts at the beginning of the play.

I'll tell my secret. I'll tell why I'm good at what I do, at easing people out of life. Ready? I don't pity them. Tenderness, yes. Pity, no. Pity is something we feel for the poor. The weak. Pity implies that we are stronger, more able, that we can afford this remorse at someone else's suffering because of the safety of our superiority. Very few people want to be pitied for long. A person who deserves pity can do nothing but ask for the mercy, the help, of those who pity. No one wants to have sex or do a business merger with someone they pity.

You're not going to name your baby after such a person. And believe me, to the very end, that's what we want, we humans. Sex and power and money and to be remembered as sexy and powerful and someone to be emulated.

Compassion, sure. But you won't get pity out of me. It was a life. You did what you did with it. Now you are on the way out. With the dying there is a focus, a bit of time to celebrate or to mourn and then: over. Sucks, but there you go.

I can do it with the dying, no pity. No problem. But the living, those still wandering around after the death, cut loose, they are lost in the woods and I don't know what will happen in their story before the end and so I fall into pity. That's why I don't do the living. No funerals. Frank. My God. The man was existing in a dark, half-unpacked apartment with his stuffed wife. It was pity that made me ask him to racquetball. I could tell because I didn't want to go. Some people like the heady power of pity. Not me.

So the sports goggles helped.

Frank played decently.

"Play a lot of racquetball in the Tupperware world?" I asked.

"Reusable food storage," he started. Then he said, "Yes. A little."

Standing in the service zone, he said, "I laid her down this morning. I eased the skirt out of her fingers and I looked to see, well, how anatomically correct she was. Everything was stiff. It bulged too much." Then he smashed the ball against the front wall.

We played in silence for the next half-hour. Only the sound of our shoes squeaking and the puckered noise of the rubber ball against our rackets and the walls. Occasionally Frank hit the ball at a funny angle so it made a sound like a water droplet falling into a pool. Each time it happened he smiled.

I don't think the dead experience purgatory. Only the living.

Marjorie called. I almost refused to go because what the hell was I doing sharing hobbies with people who hung out with the corporeal remains of their spouses. But George wasn't really dead yet and

I didn't think Marjorie could make it much longer on the no-food routine.

I got to the nursing home early and when I walked into George's room Marjorie had her humped back to him, a Pop-Tart in her hands. What do you do? It's like catching some guy looking at porn in a library. I coughed.

"Oh. Hello, Honey." She looked at the shiny foil. "Yes. This. Someone left it here." She brushed at her lips nervously.

We said nothing as she circled the room, pushing herself off the edges of furniture, trying to find a place to put the food. I thought of squirrels hopping this way and that with nuts in their paws, looking for good hiding spots.

Finally she stopped shuffling around and turned to me. "I feel like I'm not supposed to be able to go on," she said. "We married when I was seventeen. Seventeen. You know, sometimes I think about my body growing old but it is his body, the changes in his body, that I see."

Leaned into the bend in my elbow, Marjorie made her way back to the bed. We sat together on the pieced quilt. After a moment she turned toward me and I could see her paper cheeks were wet from tears.

"The thing is, I think I can live without him."

I could have left. I wasn't billing. There would be no dying. But I stayed for her to slaughter me a few times at checkers. On the way out she handed *La traviata* back. I put my palm on George's forehead to say good-bye.

I didn't hear from Frank for a week and then I got a voicemail.

"Sally. Frank. We played racquetball. Well. Here's the thing. Rachel. I believe I had spoken to you about how I started to think, really, about her internal organs? Yes. Well. I've cut her open, you see. I guess I wanted to know. I pulled everything out and, well." There was a long pause. "Sally. I don't know what to do next."

You can't help but look over in the dead wife corner when you go into someone's house when you know they just pulled all the stuffing out of their dead wife. A sheet lay over the ground, lumping up in places. In the cloth's print pattern, red berries accented a blue floral spray.

Frank had his glasses back on. The light reflected off of them.

"Coffee?" he asked.

"Sure," I said.

Here's something I've learned from the dying: most people, turns out, have saved a life. And most people have been saved. Some want to tell you about saving another human and some want to tell you about getting pushed out of the way of a bus by Mr. Greger when they were ten. Turns out some people think it amazing that they stepped in to help another being and the others still wonder that anyone would make an effort to keep them from death.

We sat on the couch, the sheet across from us. Rachel's clothing had been moved away. Frank's body, heavier than mine, depressed the cushions and I braced my feet and legs to not slide into the gulf.

"It's funny," he said. "When I pulled everything out, the foam, whatever, when I was holding it, I thought, 'Heart.' 'Kidney.' 'Gallbladder.' I felt each part in my hand. Perfect. And when I dug in again, each time, I felt the warmth of her blood, the softness of tissue swelling up around my fingers. Perfect. I loved her. You know. It made me crazy, sometimes, that I could not crawl all the way inside her. That I could not know her entire body."

In the hospital Rachel had told me how Frank's love, when they met, was complete and safe. How it had become stifling. Then she kissed me.

I make a job of not saving lives, of letting the story unfold while I watch. There, sitting next to Frank, I saw that the marvel of all that saving and being saved that people experience is not the act, not that I or someone else would climb into the burning car, but that we could pull each other off the train tracks, step forward and change the story not because of pity, but enticed by care and responsibility.

"Now I feel like I've known her totally, her flesh," Frank said. He began to cry. He set his coffee cup on the ground. "I'd taken another woman out for drinks. At the conference. Just before I got the call about," he started to gesture at the sheet and then swung his hand around over his head, indicating no specific place.

On the way to the forest preserve I stopped at a hardware store for a shovel. The whole drive Frank cried.

I sliced into the ground with the blade. After a few minutes watching me dig in silence, Frank began to sing. Frank had a lovely voice. Tenor. He sang while I dug. *You are my sunshine, my only sunshine.* In the end, the hole was not clean and squared but lopsided and rounded at the bottom where I got tired. We put the sheet and Rachel in the grave. Frank laid origami paper down the length of her body, a rainbow of diamonds, each piece kissing the corner of the last, and took the shovel from me and began to pile the dirt back on the remains of his wife.

HOLY PALMER

Edwina pressed the button next to the back door of the church. The harsh buzz, like metal tugged around the edge of a rusty cog, reverberated inside. After a while the oak door swung open and a man in a sweater and tie stood before her. She guessed he was maybe sixty, maybe twenty years older than her, though she often found it hard to know the age of Americans.

He looked at Edwina and then down at the baskets next to her feet.

"The palms," she said.

"Oh good," he said.

Their words stumbled over each other.

Then he said, "You've arrived." He held out his hand. "Russ. I'm a lay minister."

Edwina put her hand in his and left it there while he shook it.

"Edwina," she said.

Russ bent down, grunting a little, for the baskets.

She knew she should get on the bus, go home, collect the stacked baskets of palm fronds looped into crosses, take them and sit outside of her train station, sell them for a nickel a piece. This would be her best sales day of the year, the crosses laid out next to her everyday products, palm frond kittens and bears. People heading in and out of the train station, guilty for not being at a church, compelled by the weight of Jesus's impending suffering, would purchase her crosses, handfuls of them, to take home or to put in their pockets during work.

"I can help," she said.

"Oh. Thank you." He picked up three baskets overflowing with thin palms arching lazily over the sides and she picked up the other two, filled with crosses made of woven fronds, the baskets light and large. They made their way through the church and Russ chatted at her and she responded as best she could in her new English.

"You are a long way from home?" he asked.

"No," she said. "This is home now."

Life had prodded her northward as if she were a ball floating on the ocean's surface, the tides and waves lapping her farther and farther out to sea. She and her husband eventually bumped against the U.S. border and then, after bobbing there for a while, walked days and nights through the desert and continued north.

Later he asked, "Are you married?"

"No," she said. Her husband had died in an emergency clinic a year before, a year after their trip through the desert, his heart unable to perform its duties.

"Me neither," he said. "Or, not anymore."

They arranged the baskets of palms next to the entranceways to the sanctuary. Edwina enjoyed the rustle of leaves in the velvet-and-marble silence.

"Stay for the service," he said.

Russ had hazel eyes the color of the hills around the city in late summer, when the grasses started to dry and crackle and lie down flat against the earth.

"Okay," she said.

When the service ended, everyone out lining the sidewalk where the choir had walked, palms in their hands, Russ invited her to the church parlor and they ate small sugar cookies from tangles of plastic grass and drank cups of coffee. Russ introduced her to parishioners, people chatting, circled into knots. He broke apart the tight groups to say, "This is Edwina. She joined us for the first time today."

"Welcome," the people said.

Edwina nodded her head. The groups recinched when she stepped away.

Once, when he brought her cream for the coffee, she touched his wrist. Twice he put his hand on the small of her back to guide her through the room. She watched children sit on the floor, tired of their pretty lace dresses and starched slacks, unweaving her crosses, stripping the fronds down into leathery ribbons.

He offered her a ride home.

"Thank you," she said.

Normally she would have said no, taken the bus, but when he asked, "I'm driving home. Can I give you a ride?" an enormous exhaustion flooded her body and she could hardly stand and after she said yes she could hardly move her legs, so heavy, stone and iron.

The air in his car was chilly.

"Here," he said. "Heated seats."

They made comments about the weather. They talked about birds and described to each other the people they saw through the windows.

"I'm going home to eat lunch. Would you join me?" he asked.

Edwina closed her eyes into the exhaustion that had become delicious. She felt how far she had sunk into the warm, smooth seat.

"Yes," she said.

They ate tuna salad with pickles on large pieces of toasted bread. He spooned the tuna salad from an opaque plastic container he retrieved from the refrigerator.

"I made this yesterday," he said. "I'm always hungry when I get home from church."

After they ate they stood next to one another at the sink, circling water over their plates, handing the dish cloth back and forth, the cups, the spoon. She ran her finger wrapped in the soapy cloth around the ridge in the plastic container where it snapped onto the cupped lip of the bottom section. She watched water drip off the plates, out of the dish rack, while she dried her hands. He touched her shoulder and then, when she looked up, he touched her wrist. In his hazel eyes she saw square flecks of gold. Scalloped-edged circles of deep brown ringed his pupils like a child's drawing of the sun and a fan of deep cut lines ran back from each of his eyes and she thought how much hard work he must have put into smiling throughout his life.

They took off one another's clothes and fell asleep together in his bed. When it was dark they woke and Edwina felt refreshed and sluggish. They caressed each other's bodies slowly and he ran his lips over her shoulders and breasts and licked her nipples and belly and down between her legs. She put her hands on his head and rocked her hips and then pulled him up and kissed him and they made love quietly, with passion but without urgency, as if they had been sharing a bed for years.

Russ invited her to stay and Edwina thought about the stack of baskets filled with palm crosses waiting by the door to her room, about the palm fronds waiting to be shaped into rabbits, boxes, puppy dogs, about her daughters who did not want to come north, wanted to stay with relatives and husbands and boyfriends who lived back along the trail that had brought her to America and asked to be taken home.

She said, "I will see you at the church."

When she entered her room it felt more spacious. There was more room for air. Through the week she took breaks from weaving, stood in the middle of her room and closed her eyes, stretched her fingers into the vast expanses around her. She allowed herself to feel giddy.

"Russ," she said and rolled the first letter along her tongue, against her teeth, like a purr and the last letter seeped out in a long sigh.

The next Sunday she returned to his church, arrived just before the ceremony started, and took a seat in the back pew, in her pocket a palm-frond frog she had made while thinking of Russ. She stood and sat and stood and kneeled with the congregation, the rhythm of the ceremony, if not the words, familiar from childhood. She did not see him. When it came time to pray for the souls of the sick and the dead, she heard the cantor say, *Russ*, one sharp sound. In the parlor after the recessional, everyone smiled, for Christ had risen. Edwina found the priest.

"Russ?" she asked.

"You were here last week, weren't you?" said the priest.

"Yes."

"I'm sorry. Russ passed away on Monday."

"Passed away."

"Died. A stroke."

"Stroke."

"Yes. His brain."

The priest did not put his hand on her shoulder to comfort her and she was relieved she did not to have to endure the weight from his body.

"The funeral is tomorrow."

She did not understand most of what they said at the funeral. In the pew in front of her a teenage couple whispered through the ceremony. When the congregation processed forward to see Russ for the last time, the boy said, "I've never seen a body before."

"Me neither," said the girl.

Edwina wondered how they knew Russ and who could be so old and never have seen someone dead.

There was a program printed on vanilla paper. On the front it said Russ's name and *To deliver their soul from death and to keep them alive in famine* and *I go to prepare a place for you. I will come back and take you to be with me that you also may be where I am.*

She went home and did what she had done her whole life whenever anyone died, cousins, brothers, her father, grandparents, aunts, friends, neighbors. She took everything that reminded her of Russ and burned it.

When her husband had died she filled up two suitcases and a several plastic grocery bags with his clothing, the sprigs of purple flowers he gave her, dried and pressed between sheaves of tissue paper, photos, the dollar crime stories he liked to read, his pillow, and hauled them, her back aching and fingers turning plump and red where the plastic grocery bag handles wrapped around them, to a thin strip of sand next to the ocean. She dumped the remnants of her husband's life out and turned her back to the wind, cradling matches to her belly, shoulders humped. After she sheltered the fire long enough for it to spread, after watching it curl back pages and magic delicately expanding holes into work shirts and jeans and the plastic bags, Edwina took the suitcases to the water and filled them with waves. She dug up handfuls of sand and scrubbed the insides of the cases, rinsing and scrubbing and rinsing and scrubbing until the fabric linings began to tear and her hands burned in the salt water. She propped the luggage open to the fire and lay down as close to the flames as possible. When the last embers turned gray and the wind scattered the ash out over the sand, Edwina closed up the suitcases and carried them home, their empty bodies rattling against her legs.

For Russ, she sat on the floor of her small, rented room and burned the palm crosses left from the week before. She lit each one over a steel cooking bowl, held it until her fingers started to singe and then touched a match to the next one. Each time she felt tears break through the soot on her face and clean a track down to the skin she reached into the bowl and dammed the tears with a smear of ash. After the last cross burned she was weary from the smoke and the sorrow. She placed the frog she had woven for him on top of the ash and then lay down, cradling the full bowl to her stomach, and cried till she slept.

When Edwina woke she burned the frog.

"Done," she said.

If she kept things from her husband, the cousins and brothers and all the dead, her room would be full, with no place for her to live.

She went to a bustling hospital after a few months to make sure she was pregnant. She waited in the exam room for the tired doctor, her lab coat saggy with books and pens, to come back.

"You are pregnant," the doctor said.

Edwina thought about a time, before they crossed the border, when she had gone to a clinic set up in an empty schoolhouse and run by foreigners who came south to work for a few weeks at a time. Edwina was twenty and had had two children and two miscarriages. She did not want to be pregnant again, did not want another child, did not want to worry about her husband, who would love the child, bounce it on his knee and let it ride on his shoulders, but also complain about the expense and that breastfeeding made her so skinny. She went to that clinic pretending to need confirmation of her pregnancy, answered questions about menstruation and peed in cups. The young doctor, in a t-shirt and jeans, smiled so happily, "Congratulations," she said in faltering Spanish, "You are pregnant." She continued to smile, full of joy and Edwina tried to stop but broke down crying. The doctor looked confused and slightly panicked. Edwina wondered if that were the first time the doctor had ever told anyone they were pregnant.

Edwina tried to explain that she didn't want it. Wasn't there something they could do? Something safe?

"No, no," the foreigner said.

Here in this bright American hospital the tired doctor with the slumped shoulders said, "You are thirty-nine with a history of miscarriages. Do you want to keep the baby?"

"Yes," said Edwina. She rubbed her belly and thought, "My little frog."

Until the end of the pregnancy Edwina still climbed up a palm tree once a week at 3am to harvest fronds. She had started weaving palms just after they settled in the city, when she and her husband spent each day looking for work. Once she helped a woman up the hall weave Palm Sunday crosses for two cents a cross. That night she took some of the fronds home and taught herself how to work them into boxes and then little tables and stick figure humans and then bears and doll houses and tulips. She set up a blanket outside the nearest train station and sold her figurines for as much as she could get. She took requests from the police and made their wives and husbands and children delicate models and no one said anything about a vendor license. In heavy winds she had to pick up the corners of the blanket, all the figures clattering together, to keep her work from blowing away. Sometimes a man selling CDs laid a blanket next to hers, sometimes a woman who sold wool hats. With other odd jobs here and there she got by, enough to rent her room and eat.

When she climbed she hugged her body to the lower leaves, dry and sloughing off, and cut tufts of the limber green fronds that grew above. Generally she went up the low, squat palms with long combs of branches, the ones that dotted wealthier neighborhoods. She carried her palms home and kept them in buckets of water along one wall of her room. Throughout the week she selected fronds, testing their thickness and elasticity, and wove the figures in her imagination.

After he was born, she and Walter lived together in the room she rented. In the evenings she sang and wove palm fronds while he played on the floor with scraps of the leaves. During the day he stayed with a neighbor or came with her while she sold the figures. He had hazel eyes and she called him Frog. When he started to talk, they played a game where he asked her to make things, "Mama, can you make a dog?" "Mama, can you make a truck?" "Mamma, can you make a dragon?" "Mama, can you make a triceratops?" and then Edwina spent some time thinking about how to bend and tie the fronds and eventually presented him with a dog, a dragon, a tractor, a dinosaur. Frog played with the figures, staging battles and building empires, until they became frayed and started to crack in on themselves and he returned to his mother to ask, again, "Mama, can you…"

He went to Even Start and Head Start and Kindergarten. She took English classes. She thought of going back south but then thought about his citizenship and education. A woman who wore jewelry made of large stones and who owned a boutique started selling Edwina's figures. The sign next to them said they were made of organic fibers and every time someone purchased a tulip or a picture frame, Edwina made ten times as much as she did when she sold from the blanket. She thought of moving them into their own apartment.

Sometimes Edwina woke the Frog in the early morning to come and watch her cut palm branches. It was his favorite thing she could give him. He watched, always in silence, while she attached a rope to one ankle, passed it around the side of the tree opposite her body, and tied it to her other ankle. He watched her use the rope to brace herself as she accordioned her way up the smooth trunk, arms clinging, knees bending and stretching out again and again. He ran to catch the strips of palm she cut down and giggled when she said hello from the high branches.

One night just before second grade started he begged her to let him climb a tree.

"Only a little way," she said. Edwina tied the rope to his ankles and was surprised how quickly he inchwormed up the tree. In only a few seconds he started to move away from where her arms could reach, and she said, "Come on down, my little Frog." When he whined, she said, "Now," and he went limp and let her slide him down the tree. She helped him untie the rope from one skinny ankle. "Take off the other one, Son," she said and turned to collect the palms. After she had them piled on the ground she would bind them together with the rope.

He screamed for just a second as he fell. At the sound she knew he had not listened to her and had scurried up the tree once again. When she got to him there was no blood. His fractured skull and his arm and leg bones, twisted into dizzy shapes, had not sliced through him, as if his thin, soft child skin had been far stronger, more resilient than the fragile bones it encased. The end of the rope she had tied to him still bound his ankle and the other side remained palsied in the rings of the knot he had retied too loosely. His eyes looked up at her, dull green.

For days she worked to weave a figure of her son out of fronds. When she finished it was the size of a boy, perfect with each finger and toe. Frog, she called it and it hardly weighed anything. Edwina laid it in her bed each night, slept next to it until early one morning, after it had dried pale and brittle, she rolled against the boy, crushed it and woke to the fronds slicing into her arms and face. The next day she took the pieces and scattered them near his school and began to weave a new boy.

IF LOVE BE THE MOTHER OF INVENTION

Our great-great to so many powers was a man who wished to hold a woman. He had no property he could call his own or ask a wife to and so he wandered, as a minstrel, through gnarled forests and along roads that deceived his ankles to twist down holes and his toes to catch on stones. He hoped for the trees, the lanes, to open into the next village so that he could have a warm bed and feel the press of welcoming handshakes. His joy was the accepting ears of people who rarely heard news and songs. Like explorers who looked up and saw great mountains pillowing toward the sky, he fantasized hills he traveled between villages to be the voluminous breasts of a sleeping woman, trod across her wet-leaved hips, his rough feet pausing, seeking the gentle rise of her breath. This lonely minstrel, our great-great, found, in a sleepless midnight shadow, a hollowed tree stump. It was light enough to lift up and cuddle, curved so that he nestled his hand into its waist and with a hole in the belly around which he longed to run his fingers. Like sailors who saw long, flowing hair in knots of kelp, the flash of milky skin and tapered waists when dolphins leapt beside their ships, the minstrel imagined onto his stump the face of a woman. He stroked the wood, soft from age, down where he felt muscles stretching out to grip hip bones. He gently patted the round of her backside and the log answered him with quiet notes thrummed out from the hole in the center. The lonely, wandering minstrel began to sing a song to the log. He thrilled high and wavering, pushing his sweet voice to the edge of its range and, then, pressing the log against his chest, one hand at her waist, the other cupped to her breast, plunged down into base notes. He gasped when the log trembled in response. Along the smooth of her stomach he lightly tapped a finger, keeping time, and then used the flat of his hand and struck her with his knuckles and heard her sing along, heard her hum, click her tongue, beat a foot in rhythm with his song. Ah, he thought, what a pair we will make, our sweet voices wrapped around each other all day and our bodies all night. They sang till dawn lit the sky and then he fell asleep, bound around her.

When he awoke there was, next to him, a log, hollowed by ants. It had vague curves and a hole at its center where, long ago, a branch had fallen away. He took it with him and for days carted it around, singing and tapping against it. The music pleased the people. He came to think of the log, always, as *her*. He discovered that, if he plucked the rope tied to keep her on his back, she sang out. So he tied more ropes. At night he unbound her and ran his hands over the smooth grain of her skin. He peeled away bark to expose fresh, moist wood. He heard, in the whisper of his fingers upon her surface, moans that answered his own. During long days on the roads, her smell, like earth and baking bread, remained on his hands. Eventually, though, her waist and hips seemed to lose some of their youthful firm and her breasts were not as appealing. He dreamed of other logs.

To bury such thoughts, the minstrel held her hard all night and pulled fiercely at the ropes, sang desperately. But while he walked the broken country roads the log weighed heavy on his back. Eventually he told himself that she sang flat, that her skin had become dry and bleached and reminded him of a dying thing, that he could do better. His caresses became half-hearted.

He searched the woods, leaving the old log waiting at crossroads, going deep into dales and following faint deer paths until they ended in thicket, but could find no better log. The only thing to do, he felt, was to make his own. The minstrel paid carpenters to thin wood he delivered from the forests, soaked the boards in rivers until they became pliable and worked them into crests and valleys. He put a neck and a head on his engineered log, so he could feel her solid form when he brushed his fingers against her lips and eyelids as she slept.

He pegged ropes into his new log, like the cords of a throat. Then she was done and he ran his hands all over her, dipping his fingers into the hole in the center to feel the close air in the darkness inside, lingering his thumb along the ridges of her pelvis. That night, he took his old log and, for the last time, eased her down from his back, lay her next to a stream. He untied the ropes around her and, though she had come to disgust him, kissed her shoulders. Placing his hands flat on the small of her back, our great-great murmured a thank you and a goodbye. He murmured them again in a song.

For three nights the minstrel slept, touching his new-built log with only the outer edge of his hand, and on the fourth he gathered his courage and he gathered the wood and sang. He tapped against her and plucked on the ropes, touching his fingertips to the arteries contracting on her neck and sang of men who find love in clouds and in the laughter of rivers. He sang of devotion and of home. He cast his eyes up at the tall, slender trunks around them, he sang that he had created perfection and so nothing, nothing could cause him to falter, nothing could sour their harmony.

EVERYTHING WE LEARN WE LEARN AGAIN

Jimmy's half paralyzed from the snakebite and Shasta's disappeared and soon we'll be evicted. Mostly, though, we don't talk about any of that stuff. We get pretty far just talking bullshit.

"Corn," said Jimmy. "My only pleasure. Sis, ease my suffering."

It was one of the first days where you could really remember how hot the spring and summer would get, the air pushing in on you, and how expensive it is to turn on the AC. Jimmy gets on about this guy that sells corn and tamales. Everyday the guy clatters a shopping cart up the sidewalk and into the parking lot of the Rancho Lago Apartment Living here, where I've been crashing with Jimmy and, before she went, Shasta. Jimmy moaned till I went to buy corn.

Apartment complexes stretch out over the desert here and no one walks, except I've been thinking about doing it because of the gas prices, so you'd notice the guy, even without his rattling cart. He's short, shorter than me, Spanish, Mexican, I guess, and has a big mole that is more of a mole than a beauty mark next to the left-hand side of his mouth. His sales are real good.

"Take money from my wallet," Jimmy said.

It doesn't matter where the money comes from at this point. Jimmy's wallet. My purse. We're real broke. All cash is our cash.

I went out. I squeezed the bills and did the multiplication again and again in my head, how many corns we could get before the money goes and then counted the days and which would happen first, no more cash or us getting evicted from this apartment with most of the walls just cinderblock and the cinderblock and the woodwork and the sinks and everything painted and the paint gone yellow. I thought we'd be evicted first.

Money is a thing with us. Jimmy and me. We don't talk about it. Three years ago, after high school and my wedding, I lent him some, a few thousand. A whole lot. He's never paid me back. When he gets on to asking to spend money for the corn, a dollar-fifty, I think what he owes me. He does, too. Still, he can have the corn because he's suffering and has the gift of smooth talking and I have the gift of wanting to please people. That's what Shasta says. She has the gift of wanting to take care of people, including herself, which is very different from wanting to please them. We are triplets.

If I hesitate about the corn Jimmy says, "Come on, Lon. No biggie. Don't worry. There's options."

I am not ready for those options.

When I got married I left Jimmy and those options. But now I am back. And Shasta is gone. And Jimmy is half paralyzed and it's like those options are sneaking in and I catch them at the corner of my eye but I pretend like I don't see them. I'm trying to look at other possibilities. We'd been selling exotic insects and cactuses we found out in the desert but that was over and Jimmy's always been the one with the ideas.

I told the corn man, "Completo," like Jimmy had instructed me. When I go out there, if no one else is outside, I feel the large, blinded apartment windows looking down and if there is a group of people around the corn man talking Spanish I smile at the ground and mumble.

The man, each time, holds up a pointed wooden stick in one hand and a Styrofoam cup in the other.

"Stick? Cup?" he asks.

"Cup."

I am unprepared, each time, for the efficiency with which he tongs an ear of corn from his cooler, skewers the cob, slices the kernels off in thick, even slabs, funnels them into a cup, squeezes in mayo, butter and cheese, his foot jammed against one of the cart's wheels to keep the whole thing steady. He tilts his head towards a hot pepper shaker, "Yes?"

"Yes," I say.

He pops in a plastic fork.

I like that he asks every time about the cup and the hot pepper. I like that he doesn't assume.

I won't eat any of it myself. I don't want food out of some cooler. But I help Jimmy wipe the stray kernels off his lips if he's tired.

On the cups I draw smiling faces, like Halloween pumpkins, with the triangle eyes and nose and the mouth a moon on its back and I have a line of them on the sill between the wide Plexiglas front window and the long, dirty, swinging strips of the vinyl blind. They are for Shasta. All those smiles if she decides to come home.

After Jimmy'd had the corn, he got plastered on the end of the Jameson's and decided he wanted ice cream, like a pregnant lady or something. I said no. Too pricey.

"That's it," he yelled. "That's what we'll do. Sell ice cream. I've got the truck."

Jimmy's van is white with the windows painted over, except the driver's and the passenger's and the front windshield. He won't let me sell it because he says it keeps our options open. He knows it scares me to close down options.

"We'll need the song," he said and hummed the first line of the jingling song that ice cream trucks play. He was all sunk down in the broken couch, his good arm waving around. "Get the speakers on the roof. And the tape player. Some double D's. You're so good at that kind of thing, Sunshine."

My hair is blond. Jimmy and Shasta are brown headed. I hate when they call me Sunshine.

I said, "No market." I knew I tried to sound like Shasta, level and flat like a rock wall. But if Shasta had been there she would have turned around and walked out of the room, not even saying anything. "Don't let him start with you," she always tells me.

"It's the desert," he said. "It'll be one-ten in a few weeks. So much fucking sunshine and blue skies. Everyone's the market."

"License?" I said.

He snorted. "Gotta do something, Lon. Ice cream's not a bad option."

That's the thing with Jimmy. He wants to be more than just some low-end dealer. I want that too.

The next morning he was sober and still on about the ice cream.

I told him, "It won't work."

He said, "You scream. I scream. We all scream, Baby. It's great."

"No," I said.

"Vanilla cones. Chocolate cones. It's the option."

I went out and put the speakers up on the top of the van. Like in high school how I fixed all the crappy stuff Jimmy tried to fence. When you have been one way 22 years it is hard to be another way.

Jimmy flipped open his phone and called around to some bastard and when I came back from buying the cartons of ice cream, 2-for-1, almost all the cash, I found him grinning and shaking a cassette with his good hand. On a white sticker smashed onto side B someone had written, "ICE" in pencil.

"Let's get 'em, Champ," he said.

I wiped out an old, blue Coleman cooler and filled it with ice cubes from the tray in the freezer and the ice cream and sat it up in the back of the van and dropped boxes of cones and a 99-cent store plastic scoop between the seats. I said things under my breath about this being a better option. Everyone loves ice cream. I like ice cream. I popped the tape in the player Jimmy had found a few years back at a thrift store that now lay down amongst all the cones and stuff and pulled out into the street.

It was 3pm. School was out for the day. 85 degrees. I had the wide street to myself and I thought of all the kids and parents on the inside of all the apartment complex walls that stretched before and behind me. I imagined kids hearing the music, running out of gates, climbing those stucco walls, shouting to stop me, cash and sweaty coins in clenched fists, scoops of ice cream and rent and Shasta home again. Everyone loves ice cream. Even during times of economic hardship.

"Now," I whispered.

I hit play. Some eerie, strange sound vibrated down through the roof. Nothing jingly and happy. It took a second and then I recognized the song. "Oh Little Town of Bethlehem."

Over on the edge of the empty street I stopped and I put my head down on the steering wheel and listened to forty-five minutes of Christmas carols. By the end the batteries started to fade and "We Wish You a Merry Christmas" came out slow and gurgling.

I called.

"What we have here is an opportunity," Jimmy said. "You have to exploit it."

Jimmy liked to say this. He said it when he found the Homecoming Canned Food Drive cans and got me to load them into his truck. Then we got caught and he managed tears about our hungry family and I felt shame. They did, though, let us keep some of the cans and we ate everything in them.

"Yeah, an opportunity," I said. "Why don't you just tell me the name of those bastards that sold you this shit."

"Can't you be creative for a second?"

"You told me it would be ice cream truck music. How would you like to be driving around blasting "What Child Is This?" Who's gonna come buy anything? Some shitty Casio recording." I started singing at him through the phone, slow and nasal. I was feeling righteous anger, like when we were five and he told me that if I cut the hair off Ms. Oinks it would grow back thicker. Nothing feels as good as that kind of anger and I had this pleasant surprise when I found I knew all the words to the song so I really got into it around, "This, this is Christ our Lord."

"Shut up," Jimmy said and I began "O Holy Night."

He raised his voice over me. "No biggie. Everyone hates that 'Do your tits hang low' bullshit. Here we got something new. Christmas with your ice cream. Christmas Cream. Good. Christmas Cream. I'll paint it on the van tomorrow."

He joined in the song. Even over the phone, warbling and taking his voice up squeaky high and then down deep, I knew he was doing an imitation of our elementary school sports and music teacher.

I tried not to, but I smiled. I made a gesture of throwing something lightly through the windshield and stopped fighting. Then we gave it our all for, "Fall on your knees. O' hear the angels' voices."

"Now get out there and sell some ice cream," he said and hung up.

Jimmy and I had transitioned out of the exotic insects and cactuses because of the snakebite and the economy. And after Shasta left.

There hadn't been a license for the exotics, either, but I'd felt good about the idea. Like Jimmy had said, everyone over-waters cactuses. The scorpions, too, don't last long. We thought people would always need replacements and they would always want the next designer species. I had talent with setting traps and finding three-hundred-dollar barrel cactus wedged up against rocks. I also handled the lonely park rangers. It turned out we were small-time and when the economy went Jimmy's connections dried up. Now, though, over the phone, to whatever bastard he's trying to press, he says we gave it up out of concern for the environment.

When we were real little, Jimmy like to invent couch-cushion forts, to design them and talk them out. I built them. Shasta stood by to make sure Jimmy didn't convince me to do something that might get me killed. "Don't climb on the entertainment center." "Don't make the drop." Now she's not here.

Christmas Cream. Sure. Why not? But we couldn't afford paint.

Back out the second day, new batteries in the tape deck and the sun through the glass made me sweat but it wasn't so bad. The whole thing was new. I didn't mind "The First Noel." A bunch of times I thought maybe that I had seen Shasta out of the corner of my eye and, each time, for a second, I'd feel kind of choked and joyful.

One guy did flag me down. He was skinny and wore a suit.

"Where's Jimmy?" he asked. "It's his van."

"Would you like to buy some ice cream?"

"Tell him Miffer says, 'Hey.'"

"OK. Ice cream?"

"What?" he seemed to notice me for the first time.

"I'm selling ice cream."

"Where?"

"Here. Now."

"Out of the van?"

"Yeah. Vanilla and chocolate."

"Chocolate, I guess."

I climbed back and opened the cooler. I could see his forearms on the open window, hands lolling into the van, and thought how easily he could get in and drive the van and me away. The gallon cartons sloshed around in the melting ice and the ice cream scooped out more in slabs and chunks than the smooth ball I'd hoped for. The van engine chugged and I smashed the pieces down into the cone. Clambering into the front, cone held aloft, I watched for his hands to retreat as I scooted my legs under the steering wheel, edging into the seat.

"Two dollars," I said.

"What? It's not packaged."

"Fresh scooped."

"Is that even healthy? Tell him Miffer says, 'Hey.'" The guy walked away.

I drove home. I got the front door open and started dragging the cooler in.

"Your phone die?" Jimmy said from his twisted sheets on the couch.

"I was driving," I said. I'd let his calls go to voicemail and then listened to make sure he was all right. I felt powerful, not answering his calls, not dialing him back.

Jimmy bit his shirt cuff like he's done since I can remember.

"I've got minutes left," he said.

The cell phones were going to be cut off in five days.

"We still have time," I said.

"No biggie. With the ice cream money we'll keep one," said Jimmy.

"We should probably hang on to this one." I held up my phone.

"That one?"

I looked at the ground. "It's newer."

I thought that Shasta would call me before she called Jimmy.

"We'll see," he said.

"This one," I said. "Oh. Miffer says, 'Hey.'"

"Fuck."

"Jimmy?"

"No biggie. You can take the gun. I said it before."

"I'm selling ice cream, Jimmy. Ice cream."

"Sure. It's fine. Anyways, we've got options."

"Ice cream," I screamed.

He flipped his phone open. Then he closed it.

"She's fine, you know," he said.

We don't talk about it but we've got that thing, like you hear about with twins and stuff. We know when something is really wrong. That's how I came back. Shasta called me to find out what was going on the same day I called Jimmy to ask about Shasta. Ron had told me to get out. Jimmy said Shasta was being funny. Funny is what we said about Uncle Al and the lady next door and our mom when we were kids.

Shasta had stopped going to the office where she'd gotten a job answering phones by the time I moved back in and then Jimmy and I never told her what we were doing with the exotics. She didn't ask.

Her smile had become kind of vague. She worked really hard to get smiling and then starred off at nothing, forgetting to stop.

"I keep thinking I see her but it isn't her." I said.

Then I brought him a bowl of vanilla and we didn't say anything.

When I moved in Shasta found another twin bed and put in in her bedroom for me to sleep on. Jimmy kept staying on the couch. After she left her bed sat empty over against the other wall in the bedroom, sheets still perfect. Every night I lay in my bed and I couldn't sleep. When Jimmy got so that he could sort of get off the couch and limp around, he went and pushed the beds together. He doesn't do stuff like that. Move furniture. And he never said anything about not sleeping on the broken couch anymore. It's like I have one adult-sized bed now, except that when I get in I say, "I'm sorry," to Shasta and I wake up with my hand squashed down between the two mattresses. Sometimes they roll apart and drop me on the floor and one of them still smells like her.

The next day I heard the corn man rattle into the parking lot.

"Don't ask," I told Jimmy and carried the cooler down.

The corn man did some business as I rummaged around in the back of the van.

"Completo?" he asked when I stepped out.

"No thanks."

With a blue pen I wrote *Christmas Cream* on the back of an electricity bill. I drew some snowflakes falling into an ice cream cone, but it looked more like some kind of upside-down pyramid floating out in the stars. I taped the sign to the passenger's side window.

The cassette binged, "Away in a Manger," "Silent Night," "Joy to the World." I tooled along side streets and circled parks. By the second time through the tape I thought I might start being funny. No one came to buy any ice cream. I pulled into a parking lot and watched a mom push her kid in one of those baby swings with the leg holes and plastic high up around the waist like a giant diaper.

Shasta came into the park holding the hand of a little girl. I saw her from the back, dark brown hair to the shoulder, wavy and the walk, her feet high and kicked out at every step. Jimmy walks that way also, or he did before being paralyzed. I guess I do, too.

"Shasta," I shouted over "We Three Kings." Then I slid down in the seat so she wouldn't see me trying to sell ice cream out of Jimmy's truck.

I watched her through the space between the steering wheel and the dashboard. The little girl ran to the metal merry-go-round, climbed on and Shasta pushed. I didn't expect her to use her shoulders, to push so hard, and for the merry-to-round to spin fast, the child screaming happy as she came towards and away from and towards and away from Shasta.

The kid turned in the seat and, before Shasta could stop her, jumped off, arms up for a moment, and then hit the ground and rolled and came up laughing.

Still slumped down in the seat, I leaned on the horn. Shasta turned. I did not recognize the face I saw. My mind fought to make the image in front of me become the image I had been expecting. I gave up and my sister disappeared and instead there was this woman I didn't know, the mother of some little girl.

"It was wrong, Shasta, leaving like that," I said. "Leaving me here." I leaned on the horn some more. Then I turned up the Christmas tape as loud as it could go.

"Hey," said a voice. I looked out the window but didn't see anyone.

"Hey," it said again.

Down next to the van a man in full clown makeup, wig and red nose, sat in an automated wheelchair.

"Isn't this Jimmy's van?" he said.

"It's an ice cream truck."

"Where's Jimmy?"

I shifted to get farther from the window.

"You his sister? What? Did you color your hair?"

"You seen the other sister?" I asked. "With dark hair? Where?"

The white face paint and circles of pink on his cheeks and big-lipped frown obscured his expression.

"Pretty like a peach," he said. The engine of his wheelchair ground as he edged towards the van. "Didn't you tell him Miffer said, 'Hey?'"

He plunged his right hand into his sleeve.

"I'll shoot," I shouted and jerked open the glove compartment, even though I didn't have the gun.

He held a fake daisy aloft.

"Bang," he said.

"We can't find my sister," I said.

I gave him a scoop of vanilla and one of chocolate and he let me keep the flower. The woman who looked like Shasta was not in the park anymore. I sat listening to "Hark! The Herald Angel Sing" and petting the musty flower petals over my face.

"It's not going to work," I told Jimmy that night. He lay on the couch.

"There isn't any more Jameson's."

The night he got bit one of the bastards had come over. He and Jimmy had put away most of a bottle.

"Check it out," said Jimmy and reached into the cage with the rattlesnake. It was the first snake I'd caught and I'd nabbed out in the desert while it was drowsy with cold and it was no longer cold.

I said, "Jimmy, don't."

But he did and then half his body was paralyzed.

Shasta stayed in the kitchen with that vague smile on her face while I kicked the bastard out and drove Jimmy to the hospital.

Before we left I went to tell her we were going. She stood looking at the yellowed, greasy cabinet doors and said, "Keep his hand below his heart," in a dreamy voice. When we got back she was gone. The blinds were half open and the night on the other side of the window pressed against it like water against a boat.

Shasta had released the snake. The cage was empty but the lid was on.

From the couch Jimmy said, "Get me a glass, will you? There's gotta be a few fingers left somewhere. It takes me forever to get to the kitchen."

"The ice cream truck is over."

"It'll be fine. Did you do the Christmas Cream thing? I could really use a drink."

"No."

"For fuck's sake."

"The doctor said."

"I don't give a shit."

"Like Miss Oinks."

"Jesus. Not Miss God Damn Oinks again."

"They said no alcohol."

"You haven't cared yet."

He sat up, using his good arm to shift his body to the edge of the couch.

"No." I said and yanked his arm and pushed, hard, on his shoulders. He crumpled. I could feel him try to fight back and I was stronger.

"You fuck," I shouted. "I don't want you dead." I had my palms against his shoulders and one knee up on his chest. "You get ice cream. Nothing to drink. Ice cream. And it's a luxury."

Jimmy stopped struggling. A few tears came down my cheeks. I stood up so that they would not fall on him and went to the kitchen. When he was first real sick and his body didn't work I thought a lot about how heavy he was to roll around when I adjusted the sheet and when he leaned on me to get to the bathroom. I liked being able to support his weight. But this was different, that I could put my hands on my brother and push him down if I wanted. Jimmy has always been stronger than me. I dug a spoon into the ice cream and stopped being able to blame him so much for the Christmas Cream.

He leaned up against the pillow on the couch to eat the ice cream.

"How much did you weigh when you were born?" I asked him.

"Three pounds six ounces," he said.

"That's almost a pound more than me," I said. "How'd you find out?"

He shrugged. "I just know it."

"Yeah, me too. Shasta weighed the most. She ate the most. I found her birth certificate in her stuff in case I needed it for the missing person's report."

Jimmy did the annoying thing where he puts the spoon in and out of his mouth, the ice cream melting smaller each time he runs it between his lips.

I said, "Isn't it like her to have a copy of her birth certificate?" Then I said, "We should all be on that missing person's report. We should have the same death certificate. We should all have married Ron."

When I found that out, about the birth weights, about how we had different birth weights, I thought how all our lives Shasta'd worked so hard to make sure Jimmy and I had enough to eat. Then, for the first time, I thought that maybe she had not wandered out the door, had not left because she was funny or because she was protecting us. I thought that maybe she left because she didn't want to be there with us anymore. I had always thought that I could leave. That Jimmy could leave. Shasta wouldn't leave. I got nauseous and leaned hard on the counter when I signed the papers.

"Is it weird we never compared weights growing up?" I said. "Birth weights. Like we all assumed we came out the same. Even pieces."

I reached forward and grabbed his spoon. We don't eat from each other's plates, but Jimmy let me dig into his ice cream. My throat felt so hot against the milk and sugar I thought it must have been inflamed.

I fought open the sticky kitchen drawers and in one, under a mess of paper plates, was a bag of short, white candles. They had squished into imperfect shapes in last summer's heat. With a dull knife I ripped out the triangle eyes and noses and the moon mouths from the row of Styrofoam cups in the window. Into each I dropped a candle and then lit them and went outside to wait for Shasta to see the big smiles and the twinkling.

At Halloween we always had gone over to rich neighborhoods and Shasta walked up last to the doors, herding Jimmy and me before her. After we got home I'd give her handfuls of the best chocolate and she'd take it.

The empty spaces in the cups reflected into blurred and doubled shapes on the window. Slowly and then quickly the cups melted, the faces folding in. Inside the apartment smelled of chemicals. I left the crumpled cups there between the blinds and the Plexiglas window.

"What the hell? It smells horrible, Lon," said Jimmy. "Let's get some Jamison's."

"No."

"Why not?"

"This is it." I held up three ratty dollars.

"What?"

"The end. All the money."

"Jesus. Why didn't you tell me."

"You've been sick."

"Where did it go?"

"Corn! Corn! Corn!"

"I'll call a guy."

"No. No." I said. "Not yet. You're right. One more day with the truck."

He had his phone open and his thumb on the dial pad.

"Please," I said.

I'd left the boxes of cones up in the van and, in the morning, when I opened the side door they scattered up and out, cones flying all over the van. I shouted and dropped the ice cream cartons on my toes and shouted some more and hit my shin against the metal at the bottom of the van and sat down on the ground.

"No, no." The corn man was there beside me. "Is dirty." He leaned over, and I saw his big mole close to my face and he pulled on my elbow and got me sitting up on the edge of the van. A cone crunched under my ass. I started to cry. The man picked up the ice cream and put it in my lap. Then he picked up a cone that had rolled out of the van.

"Squirrel," he said.

"Ghost," I said.

"Squirrel." He pointed to small bite marks in the pale flesh of the cone.

"Ghost. My sister," I said. "My sister," I shouted, and leaned my chest against the tubs in my lap and squeezed them with my arms.

"Yes," he said. "Your sister."

I bought a cup of corn.

"Here." I gave the cup to Jimmy. He didn't say anything and took a few bites and wedged it between his torso and weak arm.

"She's dead."

"Sunshine."

"Fuck off. And her ghost is in the van."

He ran the plastic fork around the inside of the Styrofoam cup and the scraping noise made my spine hurt.

"So. That's that," I said.

"I would have, you know, felt it, I think."

"We've been waiting too hard. She's down messing with the cones." I was crying a lot by then.

Jimmy reached and touched my wrist. I went over and clung to the doorframe.

"Stop," I said and scratched the cheap paint with my nails.

The couch creaked and Jimmy heaved himself up, spilling the corn into the cushions. He tottered and then limped towards me and I thought he might smack me but instead he curled his fingers and rubbed the knuckles against my cheek.

"Maybe she's dead," he said.

"I can't stay here."

"OK."

"I can't leave."

"No."

"Come with me in the truck. Come sell the ice cream."

It took a long time to get to the van, Jimmy leaning on me. The corn man still circled and honked the bicycle horn attached to his cart. I hauled my brother up into the passenger seat and then went to straighten up the back. I whispered to Shasta. Jimmy pressed play on the tape deck and "It Came Upon a Midnight Clear" started. I backed ass-first out of the side door. When I straightened up two Spanish ladies, each holding the hand of a child, stood looking at me. I looked at them.

"Ice cream," said one of the kids.

"Oh," I said. "Right."

I leaned my head against the frame of the van and opened the cooler and imagined quick, perfect scoops of ice cream.

CHALK WALKER

Chalk Walker's favorite time is endless summer evenings where the sun creeps slow to the horizon, not dipping under until all the kids know they have gotten away with something, staying up so late, and, even after, the sky won't let go the light, the afterglow gone rose to burnt to blood blue waves up in the islands and peninsulas of clouds, all so quiet that the stars have come while he is still running the streets, unsure of why it is a little harder, then a little harder to see the grooves and ridges of the sidewalks. Chalk Walker's legs are long. Long so that it takes two attempts, look, look away and then look back again, to grasp their entire span. His arms reach down to the ground with only a little stooping. He moves as if on stilts and canes, lock kneed and elbowed, like a four-legged insect, and is not willowy, for he does not bend, but is thin and straight and rigid. Sometimes he worries he is brittle.

There was another one. That one favored ducks and blue panthers, living things that seemed about to move. They also drew intricate, winding hopscotch paths so Chalk Walker thought of jumping and skipping. That other one worked often in solid colors, the reds and dark purples that show so well, entice one to stop and admire, during the day. Chalk Walker drew still things, teapots and baseball caps. He had whites, light blue, pink at the top of his pocket. They are the colors that, on a moony night and in the first moments of streetlamp, still shine out from the cement. They are the colors muted and hidden by the sun.

Sometimes he thought of this other one as Hopscotch. Sometimes as Dawn or, when he discovered lots of animals flat on the sidewalks,

The Zookeeper. Sometimes Bob. He didn't like that name, Bob, and tried to shake it out of his head.

When Chalk Walker paused to admire something by this other one, a mermaid basking in the middle of an intersection, a pig, he wondered if that other one, The Zookeeper, felt the same as he did for his work, wondered if they woke with the vibrations of chalk against cement scratching in their fingertips, wondered if Zookeeper, Dawn, thought to just stay in today, the sheets so fresh and light, like being wrapped in meringue, but then, when they lay back to dream, long strips of clean pavement stretched out in their minds and guided their feet from the door. He wondered if, knelt down to the sidewalks, this other one, the Zookeeper, Hopscotch, also closed their eyes and let the big, dry sticks, the calcium and sulfate, clenched between fingers, move as they would, lines and shading, stories and portraits emerging as they would. He wondered if, when they, that other one, Dawn, The Zookeeper, fell down to sleep, if the sound of a million tender explosions of soft chalk breaking onto cement rough peaks washed up over them like a lullaby or screamed in their heads like a train.

Every day he meant to get up, to see the morning and find this other one, The Zookeeper, Hopscotch. Every day, exhausted by the long evenings, the long strides and squinting into the darkening cement, he did not wake up. He opened his eyes to the light already going soft and rubbed his ever-desiccated palms, rough, against his face.

It began to happen that, into Chalk Walker's drawings, his soda bottles and his cityscapes, occasionally, a cut finger crept. Once a giraffe with a bloodied leg. Sometimes he looked down and saw gleaming blades, two dimensional and thick edged. He shrugged and turned the corner but did not come back to that area till after several good rains. Once it happened right in front of his door, a bloody guillotine and a basket of heads, but when he came out the next evening, thinking to look away from the mess, they were transformed into a toy box and an Easter basket overflowing with bouncing rubber balls, painted eggs and gumdrops.

That evening he drew a body quartered and still connected to terrified horses. The next day he found an ogre, dancing, laughing, in the midst of four happy, wild stallions.

Chalk Walker drew fewer ice-cubed cups of lemonade. He lined more puppies drowning in vats of blood.

The work of The Zookeeper, Dawn, it was good. Often it was great. Every evening Chalk Walker's images were transformed. The axes severing mice tails he slipped onto the pavement became lollipops clutched in the joyful fingers of those mice, their tails returned to them and any babies that might have seemed dead and bloated were revived, chubby, and no longer jaundiced. The reshaping of his work left him relieved.

Chalk Walker pushed himself to tie women to burning stakes and machine gun villages. Fast along the sidewalk he strode, moving till he was ready to force his fingers to draw another horror. He stopped sleeping, his mind too full of blood and death, sewage canals with severed elbows floating on them. Virgin blood dripped from goblets onto the chins of flat eyed men and he shook at the thought of a thousand cats, eviscerated, and still trembling with the last of their lives, laid out on block after block of pavement.

He no longer thought to get up, sleepless though he was, and go seek The Zookeeper, go see the retooling of his horrors. He lay and waited the next summer evening. When the chalk wanted to draw a duck wearing sunglasses he forced streaks of blood to come down from behind the dark lenses, and when he found he had drawn bananas he made them become Viking ships, lost at sea, the men aboard mad and wielding heavy swords against each other. Yes, he thought. Seal up the banana skin over them or make them embrace each other, if you can.

It did not happen slowly, it happened one night when the clouds promised royalty in the sunset and the air was sleepy with humidity and barbeque smoke, when everyone had forgotten that the day could close with anything but a long summer evening. Chalk Walker went out and, on the cement at the corner, there was no dark-blue fairy with wings a paper-thin hint of gypsum. There was no hopscotch path for him to attempt with his long limbs. On the pavement there was no fix to his chainsaw. The brains and bits of skull still clung to its edges. The piked heads had not become smile-faced daisies. The day after, also, nothing had been transformed, nothing added. Nor the next.

It was, he knew, left to him to transform the sidewalks into flowers and draw in the boxes and balls spilling over. Chalk Walker tried to stay in bed, tried to ignore new poured pavement a few blocks away, tried to ignore the familiar alleyways, the sections of path that he had covered in horror. But the pull of chalk, running jagged, over cement was too much. So he went out and dug to the bottom of his pockets for dark colors that could overwhelm the iridescent of his own work.

He didn't know how to transform his drawings, could not envision the horror anything else, so he just drew new pieces on top, filling in outlines, carefully coloring to the edges so none of his old horrors could show through. Often he chalked over entire squares of pavement, blocks of bright yellow, blue, when he couldn't think of anything to draw. Sometimes he couldn't stop himself and came back to find deep-green goats with severed heads amongst the chocolate chips and frolicking penguins. These accidents made his arms and legs feel how unsupple, how ready to crack from every impact against the cement, they were.

Every day he could not stay in bed and, out on the sidewalks, he whispered his apologies, his promises, like a prayer, in time with the swinging of his limbs. If you come back I won't any more. I won't. Come back. If you come back I won't any more. I won't. Come back. But Dawn, The Zookeeper, did not and the chalk of their last drawings began to scatter away into the everyday dust of the pavement.

Each evening he circled out farther and farther, watching beneath his prolonged and shifting shadows for fresh drawings, a sign of The Zookeeper, stopping at smooth pieces of pavement to set down surfers and Chinese vases, but never finding anything from the other one, The Zookeeper, Dawn, Hopscotch.

Once, though, on a night when dark was coming fast on the edges of a rainstorm, the first rain since The Zookeeper had left, Chalk Walker swung into an empty parking lot transformed into miles of hopscotch. Though the work was fading, his breath caught at the elaborate mastery, at the grace of line and complexity of rule.

He found himself content and reverent in a game, following the rose petaled formation as it wound with ocean lapped islands and burning candles and plump easy chairs to leap to and bound over. As the winds came blowing up through his thin legs and thunder rumbled the chalk sticks in his pocket, Chalk Walker circled, tossing a piece of gravel to guide his movements in and in, an entire parking lot of nautilused hopscotch embracing him.

HISTORY

The Gods lived here when the land spread smooth as far as a man can walk in his life. The Gods played. They fought. They burrowed and dug and wrestled and warred and erected hopscotch paths for Coyote, lines of stone across the desert, to test the distance of his leap. The thrash of their bodies made the swirl of canyons running to empty into each other. Their blood and bone turned the canyon walls red and white. They made the stone flats and crumbling sand hills and raised up the pock-marked columns of rock. Most of the Gods are massive horned sheep with four human arms and hands instead of legs and hooves. There are a few red snakes the size of spring rivers and the Coyote has the back legs and ears of a jack rabbit. The earth churned and the Gods grew weary of the peaks and valleys, scored with the sheep's fingers, pounded with Coyote's back legs. We are here, now. The People. But at any moment the Gods return and what we touch they touch and so all must be as it is, unchanged, or the Gods bring retribution.

SPRINGTIME

The moth remakes the desert.

In spring the yucca bushes and the yucca trees that stand like immobile, hairy people, that keep the birds and lizards and mice from the cold and sun, reach cones and spears of flowers toward the sky. Then they wait, blooms open to the quiet desert. The moth emerges from the ground and cleans the pollen from the trees and bushes. She rolls it into a great, golden ball. She gathers up the globe and flies into the white cloth of yucca petals and lays her eggs in the most hidden cavity of a flower and then lowers the sticky ball down to top, trap, keep her eggs. The blooms wilt and all summer seeds and the new moths grow. In fall the yucca crack open and the seeds and the moths drop and burrow into the sandy earth and the desert is made again.

WINTER

It is my seventeenth winter and I have slept alone for seven years. This winter Shel comes to me in the night. Just to sleep. The first time he lies facing away, the smallest strip of his back touching mine, and does not move and does not move and does not move, and I can feel how tight he holds himself and when I wake he is gone. I know it is him on the blanket next to me because he smells of that great, giant dog that tries to sit in his lap. The dog gets its one haunch up on him and then the animal wiggles back and Shel groans and laughs and then they give up and the dog stays, as big as Shel, one leg cuddled on him. In our group Shel is the only doggy smelling man who has no woman to keep him asleep in one place.

The next time Shel comes he circles three times, shuffling stones with his feet and kicking up bits of dust so that I have to hold my breath, contract the muscles in my throat, to not cough. He lies on my blanket and it's cold enough that I've wrapped another one around me and he puts one hand against the blanket against my shoulder. The next time he touches his ankle to mine and the next he lies down in front of me. I do not reach out to him, but I think that maybe I do when I fall asleep. Perhaps he sleepwalks and doesn't know. Perhaps his is tired of lying next to his dog.

A man has touched me. In the day he acts the same as always, calls me Moth, gives me the spoonful of his food, no more, no less. I act the same, too. What happens if people know? Certainly I won't have another chance to rest with a person. Only the very young may touch the Moth. The very young rest with their parents.

MOTH

I am called Moth because I keep the desert. I eat and I clean everything into its right place. I do not work for the lizard and the bird and the termites. I keep the desert for the Gods.

TODAY

I wake with a shadow over my face and catch my breath. Perhaps Shel still lies before me in the daybreak. I ask the tips of my fingers but feel only my blanket against them, no human warmth, no rise and fall of breath.

I open my eyes and see Asias crouched over me.

"My son has rock drawn," she says.

"Hello. Good morning."

"Shut up," she says. "Do you hear me?"

Then she says, "Pur."

Asias is my sister. She has not called me Pur since I became Moth. Like everyone else she calls me Moth.

"Pur," she says again.

Tears come into my eyes. I feel giddy with how she says "Pur" like a question. She needs me. I roll over and give her my back.

"Pur."

I try to think what it is to be a sister.

"He is safe?" I ask. Her breath comes out loud, like wind in canyons.

"Yes," she says.

"He is safe."

"The same wall," she says.

I want to say, "What do you mean?" so that she will have to answer things that could hurt. I want to laugh. But I think that that a sister would not act that way and I enjoy being good sister for a moment. I know that she means it is the same wall where our brother rock drew and fell into a water hole and died, so many winters ago, before we were men and women.

Also, the Moth went to eat the wall and fell and the bodies stayed down, down in the water hole, and the people found me to be Moth.

It is funny, then, that perfect Asias's perfect son crawled up and drew and I will clean his drawings alone.

I am the good sister and turn back towards her. She picks up some small stones from the ground and rolls them between her palms. It is a gesture she does not know she makes until she sees me staring at her hands and puts the rocks back, one by one, on the earth and says, "Coyote, Sheep and Snake, forgive the error."

I tilt my head toward her in a way that looks kind and understanding, and say, "In the life we err."

I'm sure it is an error to feel so happy to have seen Asias's mistake and shame, but in the moment I don't care much about things like errors.

I lay both my hands on the ground.

"Later I eat this earth to make it clean for the Gods," I say. Then I am the good Moth and the good sister.

"Moth," she says, "will you clean away the drawings and make the rock pure for the Gods?" Her son should come and ask me. The one that errs asks the Moth.

I tell her, "I am the Moth and I make clean the rock."

All day boys and girls come to me and say, "Moth, in the night I scarred the rocks. The hands of Sheep and the legs of Coyote and the smooth belly of Snake touched there and now I marked them. Moth, will you clean away the drawings and make the rock pure for the Gods?" They all have headaches from the hot juice and look spindly on their thin, young legs.

'Yes." I say it seven times.

There is a howling tonight, of course. Every year it is like this, my busy day. One day Winter End and dancing and cactus cutting and rock stacks and the young get into the juniper juice after everyone else goes to sleep and they draw on the rock walls and the next day is shame and howling and then we flee from the summer sun to the mountains where the snows have melted. I love it. On this day everyone remembers me and they think that if I am not here for them summer will be dry and hungry with the Gods' anger.

I go to the Winter End grounds and spend the day smashing the carved cactus and kicking the rocks around to unstack them. I remember what I can of yesterday's dances and dance them backwards, my feet scraping dirt back to the place it is. I am alone and none watch me for my work is sacred and foul. There can only be one Moth.

RULES OF THE MOTH

There can only be one Moth and the Moth works alone. The work of the Moth is sacred and foul and none but the Gods may see.

The Moth remakes the earth and lives in the rage and contempt of the Gods.

When the Moth dies the People know the Moth that lives.

The errors of the People pass through the Moth and the earth returns to its pure form, waiting the touch of the Gods.

The Moth works for the People. The People must feed the Moth.

Only the very young may touch the Moth.

The one that errs asks the Moth.

TONIGHT

Tonight the moon is full and shadows from the choya and creosote break the cold light on the ground. I am not supposed to be at howlings. I eat the errors while the others howl and I am too foul and too close to the Gods for the circle. Often, though, I sneak and watch. The howlings are wonderful. At the mouth of Mouse Canyon I climb up and lie hidden in a shallow cave.

The whole group stands in a circle around the eight who rock drew. The Lead says, "Shame on your error." And it is like a tight string tearing. With one breath all shout at the eight. "How dare?" and "The error," and everyone screams and points. Asias stands very still and does not point. Her mouth moves for she must shout those in the middle down, all must howl the error, but she does not take great breaths. She whispers her condemnations.

The eight fall on the ground and wail their sorrow. Babies cry. Someone lifts up a rock and Asias shakes as if it has struck her. The Lead shouts, "Enough." Silence comes. Mothers comfort their babies. In the center Asias's son rocks back and forth. "Please," he says, "please forgive us." The other youth follow, yowling and rolling on the ground and soon the people in the circle, all the people, cry to the Gods for forgiveness. Asias's face skews, her mouth stretching empty in the moonlight. She kneels and then I see her chest heave as she begs. "Pity us. Pity us." And the error has become the error of all.

Sometimes I have my own howlings, out when I've finished eating, because rolling in the earth and screaming feels good. I do not howl for forgiveness. I do not know if the Moth, so close to the Gods and so foul, can error. Sometimes I think that perhaps the Gods don't care to forgive or punish the People for specific actions. The Gods bring drought and rain because they do.

If I can err, this thought is an error. It may also be a rule.

I am delighted with Asias's pain, this, the first time she or her children have been howled. I feel stuffed and breathless, too full with pleasure at that pain. Later I will howl to empty myself.

I walk up the canyon, rough rock touching my hands on both sides. The path spreads wider and the water hole, chiseled many humans deep, lies before me. The opening is small so the hot sun cannot sap away the water. The Gods come to the Leads' dreams and say, "Make tunnels of water." The People dig and dig holes condoned by the Gods. Children set tortoise shells out in the rain and dump the water down the holes. Now the People can drink. When the Gods return they will empty the water into their own bellies and so the People gouge the earth in honor of a time to come.

Thick black streaks burned by the sun run on the rock walls. In strips of moonlight the fresh drawings show high up, etched into the blots of darkness.

Sometimes, when there are only a few drawings to eat, I doodle my face or my body, lightly, onto the wall, just because I like to, and then smooth it away. Sometimes when I do that little rain falls. Sometimes the rains fall hard. What would the people do to me if I stopped eating the rock?

I climb the wall, searching out crannies for my toes and fingers, jamming my hands into cracks. I imagine the youth, giggling on the hot juniper juice, taunting each other to climb higher. It is easy to slip and tumble into the water hole below. I imagine my brother falling.

Finally I am up with the rock scratches. The eight have etched them in deep and it will take me a long time to eat them. It's the usual stuff. Someone drew himself spearing a sheep. Two people holding hands. A few stars. Lines that never became more than shallow columns before the dawn lit and the juniper no longer helped the young feel so hot.

I begin with the two holding hands. I grope for good footholds and a hollow for my fingers. Humming, I take a hard stone from my waist cloth and scrub the rock until the figures blur. The black burn powders off and coats my lips and chest and I breath the dust and see it flitter out on small breezes. The rock is clean, the red of thin blood, smooth. The People will think it is safe.

I wipe away the star and my feet numb a little so I climb down, sliding toes against rock to find fissures, hoping they do not house spiders or scorpions, and land, finally, on the narrow strip of earth between the wall and the water hole. The winter rains fell plentifully this year so the tunnel is filled almost to the top. My hand breaks the silver surface, ripples lap out and I pour the water over my face in cool streams, washing away the dust. I plunge my hands back in and find that I am drinking, sucking from my cupped palms. When my hands are empty I return them to the water and drink again.

I hear the sound of feet on the pebbled ground and look up, like a hunted sheep. Asias stands close.

"You drank the water," she says.

"It is sweet," I say.

"This is the water hole," she says.

"Yes. Of course. And this is the first wall I ever cleaned."

"I know." She raises her chin a little.

Neither of us says anything. I dip my hand into the hole and sip from the pool in my palm. I look her in the eye while I do it. I think of our brother. I think of the Moth before me, the one who fell into this water hole and floated down below the earth for hours before anyone thought to wonder where she was. She had not finished her job and so I did.

Asias coughs in disgust.

"Shouldn't you be at the howling?" I ask.

"Aren't you supposed to eat the rock?" she says.

"How do you know I don't and that the Gods aren't giving you a vision? To keep you from seeing what you should not. The Moth works alone."

"The Moth cleans for the People."

"Go away," I tell her.

She sits down. "It was so easy to come here. Just walk up the canyon."

"Go away," I say again.

"I've feared being at the center of a howling."

I feel again the joy at watching her son howled.

She picks up a stone and throws it into the water hole and laughs.

"You cannot eat that, can you? Cannot drink the whole thing dry and put the pebble back on the earth," she says, giggling.

In the moon I see her brows come together.

"Pur, will they punish us for that? That rock I threw in?" she asks me.

I start to answer but she says, "I feel that they will not."

"Go." And this time I am the good sister, telling her to go so that she will not say things she will regret.

"I was with him," she says.

"What?"

"I was with our brother."

The moonlight leaves deep gouges under her eyes.

"When he fell." She looks up at the rock wall. "We were both up. Scratching. Maybe something bit him. He tumbled down. His head on the rock. Down into the hole. He didn't answer when I yelled."

"I became Moth."

She shrugged. "When the Moth dies the People will know the Moth that lives."

Every night Asias sleeps cuddled with her man and her children and I lay alone hoping for a dog to visit and, of late, for a dog smelling man to lay out where the tips of my fingers could brush against him if I dared.

"Throw another pebble." I point to the hole.

She picks up a rock and throws it in. It makes a deep clunk sound when it hits the water.

"Again," I say.

She throws in handfuls. In the morning she will feel lonely, having doubted the Gods.

"How do you do it?" She points to the wall.

"I am the Moth. It is my duty. You cannot do anything."

I climb up the wall away from her and begin filing.

"That's it? You scrape it with a rock?"

Soon I hear her close to me grating a stone against the wall. I see her smiling.

I dig my stone in harder. The years and years that I live only to clean the messes, to ask and ask forgiveness for our little desires to mark and change, to imagine ourselves, even in a moment, equal to the Gods, worthy to use the earth. These years and years because Asias said nothing. She had not been howled for her error but I became Moth. The People said they saw the mark of the Gods on me. They also saw the years and years of water fouled with my brother's body, and I do not believe that only the Gods are capable of retribution.

The sound of Asias's stone stops. She hangs in the moonlight and leans forward into the wall and licks the figure in front of her. A boy with a spear. She licks it until I see shadows come over the rock and I cannot tell if they are made of her spit or of her blood.

"I eat the rock," she says.

"Clean the rock," she tells me.

I touch my tongue to the wall and grains of sand come away into my mouth and the hard rock tastes musty.

"Beautiful," she says. The moon illuminates the tears on her face. "Beautiful forgiveness," she says.

I am big. Big as Sheep and Snake and Coyote. I am Moth. I am nothing. I reach my hand out to her shoulder, feel the wonder, the warmth, of a human body. I can pull her from the wall. I am the Moth. The Moth cleans the error. The Moth returns the earth to its pure form. Only the very young may touch the Moth.

CUSTOMARY WEAR AND TEAR

One bag at
Bloomington.

That's the text I got from Ray during breakfast. He's the young man who's my boss. He's the Mid-Illinois Regional Baggage Manager and we are the only staff in the Regional Baggage Redirection Division.

My stomach soured when I flipped my phone open and read the text. I could not finish my toast. It would be a long drive.

Mom gripped the back of my chair. The skin of her hands has become very pale and cut with dark lines of shadow around where the bones stick out.

She said, "I think Chantilly could use an outing, don't you?"

Chantilly is an ancient mini poodle. Her fur is always greasy and matted and she emits various bad smells. The past few months Mom has started to say things like, "Chantilly wants to go with you today," and, "Chantilly doesn't want to stay cooped up here alone with me." She has had teeth removed from the left side of her mouth. She pants and her tongue falls out the gaps and she pulls her tongue back in and pants and pulls her tongue back in. I mean Chantilly, not Mom. Her snout is long and thin and so is her tongue.

When I got to Bloomington International the manila folder for the account bulged with a printed and binder clipped stack of emails. Ray had scrawled *FYI* across the first page in red ink. The account was a 62. A duffle bag.

Out in the van Chantilly panted at me while looking forward pointedly. She thought we should get going. I ran my fingers back and forth over the file's edges, just slow enough to not give myself paper cuts.

> Dear Customer Service Personnel,
> I appreciate the rapid rate of your response to the dilemma
> of my misplaced luggage. The contents of the bag are
> imperative. Adequate actions are critical.

The email came from Ms. Shelby Bilgue.

I could not be sure how to pronounce the name. Three-to-one I would be corrected when I got to the door and asked for her.

> Dear Ms. Bilgue,
> A Baggage Specialist will be available to return luggage at
> a specified address. Please note that our policy prohibits return
> of items to anyone other than the ticketed passenger. Also, the
> passenger must display both valid ID and proof of travel.

I was glad Ray had written this. Often no one tells customers and it makes things difficult.

> Dear Customer Service Personnel,
> I find myself unavailable. One Mrs. Elva Stiffton will await.

> Ms. Bilgue,
> Unfortunately our policy is non-negotiable. We will deliver
> to any reasonable location convenient to the passenger.

> Dear Customer Service Personnel,
> Nonsensical.

The emails went on. I stopped reading, flipped to the Baggage Destination form for the address and started the van.

I took county highways to Effingham. On the two-lane roads there are fewer cars and, so, I feel, a lowered chance of accident and, thus, death.

Everything is green except the soybeans and the summer wheat on their ways to golden.

No one answered the doorbell on the two-story, sided craftsman.

The second time I rang a voice behind me on the porch said, "I'll take the baggage. I'm Mrs. Stiffton."

She was my age, shorter, with her graying hair haloed up around her head in one of those impenetrable perms.

I told her, "I am not authorized to return the bag to anyone but Ms. Bilgue."

Mrs. Stiffton narrowed her eyes. Maybe I pronounced the name wrong.

"No. No. Shelby said you could leave it with me."

"I'm sorry."

The whole thing escalated fast.

I said, "I'm sorry," and then I was wrestling with the woman, each of us trying to yank the bag from the other. We were evenly matched until she looked me in the face and bared her teeth. That made me pause and she grabbed the duffle, hoisted it by the shoulder strap and trotted off the porch.

In the van I forged Mrs. Shelby Bilgue's signature. I hugged the steering wheel until it felt immobile.

At home Mom and I sat in our designated front-room seats, she on the left, I on the right, in a pair of high-backed chairs that have been stuffed until they are hard.

Mom said, "That neighbor boy came over and planted the zinnias. Good-looking kid. Bit liberal with the fertilizer, though, I'll tell you what. And imagine, he wanted the whole three dollars."

"You didn't pay him?"

"I gave him a fair wage. I kept back a dollar for the fertilizer."

There are no more neighborhood kids who will shovel our snow or rake the leaves.

I said, "I went to Effingham."

"Oh, yes. Wooden Shoes."

Mom specializes in the high school mascots of towns in Central Illinois.

"Duffle bag to a two-story craftsman."

"Siding?"

"Siding."

"A shame. Aluminum, at least?"

"Vinyl."

"Vinyl. Oh."

"Yes. But a good job."

"It's what killed your father."

I said, "I went by Fisher's on the way home for some milk."

I held up the half gallon.

"Only the one duffle bag?" asked Mom.

"Yes."

"Slow day."

I shrugged. Mom squinted at the ceiling as if she could see the location of the sun.

"Five o'clock," she said.

"Yes."

"Yes." She looked at the ceiling again. This was a conversation about unaccounted time. I had left that morning at eight am, driven to Bloomington and then Effingham and home, a total drive time of four hours, with stops to pick up the duffle, drop off the duffle and then buy some milk.

"Chantilly must have had lots of free time. Were you bored, honey?" she asked the dog.

"I'll start some dinner," I said.

Mom sniffed.

She said, "No, it is alright. I already put some chicken in to bake. It was getting so late."

I'd gotten a book out from the library a few days before. I had it in a drawer in my room. *FEAR: Full Embrace Anxiety Response, embracing the emotions within.* After dinner I flipped through it.

> *Chapter II, Pg. 7*
> *Open Your Arms. Bare Your Chest.*

Keeping a diary is a good way to learn about your own anxiety and overcome its negative effects.

Prompt #1: In your diary write about one thing you let make you feel anxiety or FEAR. Embrace this fear.

Hello.
I guess Hello.
I have not done this for a long time.
I don't really know what to do. A woman in her 50's keeping a diary.

Hi. How are you?

I wrote down the prompt. I wasn't sure if I was supposed to.

I'm fine. Well. No. I mean. I'm fine. But there could be improvement.

So. Hi. So. Soooo. Something that made me anxious. I can tell you right now the fact that the book is named FEAR makes me anxious. Can't look at the cover without my breathing going. Four days till I could open it. They have it at the top of every page, FEAR, so you won't forget what you are reading.
It's August 5. I guess I should say that.
Ok.
Good-bye?

I've been staring at the page.

Another prompt? Am I only supposed to do one per day? Well.
Prompt #2: What happened today?
Well, I drove to Effingham and fought with this lady over another lady's luggage. Mom wants to know about all the hours I was not at home. Does she?

Listen. After that thing with the lady. Listen. I will tell you.
Fred. He's the manager at Fisher's. And the butcher. And I went
to get a gallon of milk. And went to his office and we locked the
door and moved the coffee maker and security monitors off his
metal desk and had sex. We kept our clothes on and knocked
over a bottle of powdered creamer.
Fred would say we fucked.
This is making me hollow. Writing.
Mom says What's on your shoulder? and I have powdered creamer that fell out of my hair and stuck to my airline blazer. So I say
I have dandruff and Mom does her little sniff.

I worry I do the sniff.
I am always watching myself.
Sometimes things slip.
Ok.
Good-bye.

Chapter VII, Pg. 97
Soft Heart. Long Heart.
*The practices you have used are not just for today. Your Diary, your Candle
Ceremony, and Open Door and Dance of the Winds, all the techniques you
have learned, be empowered to use them as long as you find helpful.*

August 9th
As long as you find helpful.
I'd hoped for a more defined timeline.
But I don't start many things. So I'd like to follow through.
Prompt #3: Write about your job. Use a highlighter to identify
things you let make you feel anxious. Embrace.
I don't have a highlighter. I have to buy one. That makes me anxious.
Job. There are reasons to stay. Health insurance. Stock options.
And my pension going. Going. Lingering is important. (Highlight
that)
I didn't start out like this. With the baggage.

I was a stewardess. Our skirts were made of paper. That was long ago. Do you remember? Businessmen burned holes in them with cigarettes. Snicker like third graders. Polyester blends and comb overs. Smacking on peanuts. (highlight?)
Ok.
Good-bye

August 11.
Prompt #5: What is on your life resume?
I feel I should say that after I stopped being a stewardess and the divorce I live again with my mother. She won't leave the front yard. (highlight)
Ok.
Good-bye

August 12
Prompt #7: Trust yourself. What helps you overcome FEAR?
A long time ago I got a cassette tape. A man talking about how to relax. Low calm voice. His accent made me think of Alabama. Have you been? I have. Only the airport. All over the case and the tape it said DO NOT LISTEN WHILE DRIVING. The warning seemed unnecessary. The very first thing the man says is to close your eyes. But after a while I got so I felt hungry for the rattling of the spools inside the plastic casing. Only the thought of the car crashing stopped me from inserting the tape into the radio on the dash. One day it unwound itself. Screaming and spitting ribbon out of the deck. I tried to wind it up again and it snapped.

Sorry to disappoint. I'm not the kind that exercises or knits when I'm going to die. When my heart
Is that going to change, FEAR? I'm in my fifties.
I wish it would change.
And that's going to be true forever, too.
But I did learn some breathing. From the tape. In. Hold. Out. In. Hold. Out. In. I use that. Sometimes. When it is difficult. When it is

like that. When it is hard to get the air and have the pain in my chest. How it is possible for the front of a car to crumple and sever the shinbone from the thigh.

And the drinking. For overcoming.
Ok.

August 13
There are some things I did not say about my job. I do not say.
A Chicago-Louisville flight and I picked up the intercom phone. Hard plastic. And said to go back to your seats. The pilot expected it to get bumpy.
(highlight. Highlight all of this)
How to say? I do not have kids. I do not but when I told everyone to Please remain seated I am talking to children.
My children.
My voice in their ears.
I heard it and I heard this word. Bumpy.
Mangled bodies. All twisted.
Broken.
And heads shattered against overhead luggage bins.
Watermelons with sledge hammers.
Oh God.
I do not like this, FEAR.

The telephone was the same model as the one on the wall in my kitchen. Vanilla. Humped like half a hard-boiled egg.
It is more.
I met with a supervisor and said Isn't it so hot in here? And unbuttoned my blouse farther and farther.
Isn't there any other way I can serve the company?
The divorce and I was not going to get much.

Did I tell you about my mom's dog? Chantilly.

I spend a lot of time on the bank of the interstate with the hazards on so she can piddle.

I imagine our bodies swept away by a semi. (highlight)

I have never written that down before.

Bumpy.

It does not look right. How can it look so different from the sound? Not like terror.

Ok.

August 14

Prompt # 10. Here are two different words: 1) Family, 2) Embrace

Dad smoked two packs a day. Do you smoke? He was also an amature architectural historian. He let the siding get to him. According to some books I have read I think maybe the siding wasn't the real problem.

I do the grocery shopping and when I am a good daughter I lie about any siding I saw that day.

Here is something else.

Mom still offers me a plate of apple slices and peanut butter when I get home.

The ten years of my life I did not live with her I never bought a jar of the stuff.

I craved it every day.

Ok.

Good-bye.

August 15

Prompt #11: Imagine your diary is a letter. Who are you writing this to?

The last time I did this. The diary. I was twelve.

Mom picked the lock and found out I thought she looked fat in her new dress and that I had burned my lungs smoking leaves from the cigar tree in the front yard and that Billy Roden had put his hands all over my chest and said he was glad I didn't wear a bra.

Weeks she asked if I thought she looked fat. And about my breathing. Did it sound a little raspy.
Using concern to make you feel small.
There she excels.

Hello, Mom. How long did it take you to find this diary.
Ok.
Good-bye.

This morning Ray texted:

4 bags. Peoria.

The file bulged full of printed emails with *FYI* scrawled over the front. The emails were between Ms. Shelby Bilgue and Ray. It was the same name as the lady with the duffle bag a few days before. I counted breaths.
I texted:

Whats going on with this lady?

After a while he replied:

Who.

I called Ray.
"Yes," he said.
In the background I could hear several people talking and things falling on the ground.
He said, "Put it over there," to someone. Then to me he said, "You okay?" I never call.
"Everything's fine," I said.
I carried the bags out, one by one. 62s and 25s. Two duffels, two rollies. Chantilly whined, bored and wanting to poop, each time the back doors opened.

This time Mrs. Bilgue asked that the bags be dropped at a residence in Kewanee.

> Dear Customer Service Personnel,
> I am a woman of little leisure. If you insist on such disregard to my personal belongings, I insist that you accommodate to my geography.

There was an address.

The front door of the house, a brick, two-story neo-classical, had an ornate steelwork screen door. A note wove its way through the bars. It said:

> *At Hog Days. Please discover me in the Pig Kissing*
> *Booth or near the Tilting Teacup operator.*

The script flowed gracefully across the page, like a love letter or a declaration of war.

I left the van in the middle of the elementary school playing fields that doubled as Hog Festival parking and walked to the downtown blocks cordoned off for the main activities. I know Chantilly watched me leave.

The blocks inside the festival grounds swayed with people and smelled of roasting pork and sticky sweet garbage.

Mrs. Stiffton stood in front of the skeet-ball tent. The crowd did not buffet her, though she was short. Her hair maintained its helmet form. She opened her thin and pale lips to take a bite of cotton candy, but when she saw me she closed her mouth and silted her eyes. We took off, racing up the blacktop street, weaving around people and booths.

I don't sprint very often. My lungs burned and I could not quite catch Mrs. Stiffton.

In the field my white van covered in the airline logo stood out. Mrs. Stiffton headed for it.

"Ha. It's locked," I thought.

She got to the back of the van, reached for the handle and popped the door open and had the bags out as I still slalomed through rows of cars. One duffel stacked on each rollie bag, a rollie bag handle in each hand, her right fist also wrapped neatly around the cotton candy stick. She trotted away across the grass. Before she disappeared behind the school, Mrs. Stiffton turned and smiled.

I returned to the festival to buy Mom a funnel cake. I watched people shoot water guns into the mouths of cardboard pig faces, trying to fill and burst balloons that grew out of the top of the pig heads. A group of kids swarmed around me, screaming and laughing, all of them short enough to ignore me, as if I was a tree planted in the middle of the street, but if they had pushed I would have toppled and been swept away.

At the van I opened the driver's side door and held the inside of the doorframe and rested one foot on the running board. After a long pause I heaved myself up. My leg felt weak, trying to lift my body.

I turned the ignition and thought about heart attack. It was very vivid, the way I would slump forward, the steering wheel waggling uncontrolled.

> August 16
> I'm writing to say that FEAR is lost.
> I am not embracing the anxiety.
> It is not in the van. Not under the seat.
> Nowhere.
> I've been enough times to the hospital.
> This is panic. Not a heart attack. This is panic.
> Maybe this is what aneurism is.
> The chest pains.
> It does not help, Mom and her pills.
> Two years ago the doctor gave her the pills for her heart.
> The bottle's empty. She will not go get more. They call. To remind her.
> Just before I went through the police barriers at a town festival today a convertible passed. Slow.
> Up on the back seat was a girl. Solid. Freckles. A refitted bridesmaid dress and a sash. A banner the whole length of the car says:

Kewanee Pork Princess.
The Other White Meat

Do you know this? We give titles, princess and queen and king, to our best and brightest. Valedictorians. Future leaders. What we have for honor.

Here. Highlight this. I never had a ribbon over my chest. Corn. Dairy. None of the proud farm products.

Maybe I will make a bandage to go around my chest. Keep my heart safe.

Also.
Driving home my heart so loud. The road that will soon be icy. Chantilly panting. Panting and her tongue will not stay in her mouth.
Shut up I told her. Yelled.
Shoved her little grey tongue in with my finger. All her rotting gums and the back of her throat and she yelped and shrunk towards the door on her old old legs.

I always lock the van doors.
I swear.
I lock them and say Cross check complete.

Her whole life. Mom with these little dogs.
Chantilly could be the last.
Ok.
Good-bye.

August 18
Manito. Whip-purs. 25. Rollie bag. Brick bungalow. Nice garden.
Cobden. Appleknockers. 17. Suitcase. Sunshore Hotel.
Teutopolis. Flaming Hearts. Double wide. 9. Backpack.

Sesquicentennial fair.
Fred is well.
Chantilly did not poop all day.
She tried many times.
I am dying.
Ok.

August 19
This AM station broadcasts out of Havana.
On a clear day you hear it from Lafayette to Bethany.
Eight hours a man with a quiz show.
Retired. Maybe.
People call to answer questions or no one calls and he just reads
question after question. No theme. No answers. Sometimes he
chuckles. Private. After the question.
I shout out the answers if I know.
Sometimes the list of things I do not know comforts me.
No work today. I did not go. Heart is a little better now.
Maybe he knows where the book is. The man on the radio. Maybe
someone will call with the answer. Maybe they called today while
I stayed home.

Mom opened a notice from the library. Honey she said.
It is fine. Don't worry I said.
I do not want her worry.
Ok.
Good-bye.

August 22
Hopeson. Cornjerkers. 19. 43. Suitcase and well-taped office supply
box. Spanish revival.
The suitcase light. The box heavy.
For Ms. Shelby Bilgue but she isn't here. Neither is Mrs. Stiffton.
I have the note:

Often I have discussed the imperative nature of the objects of delivery. Strenuously, beyond all needs, I implore their arrival. I am not able to be at the pre-stated location and am aware of your policy regarding individuals to whom baggage will be returned. Thus I ask you to allow my property to find its safe path to the following address.

The address. Florida.
The score. I am losing. Losing to this lady.
Remember that life resume? The only thing I can be proud of is the baggage. The 25s, 62s, 4s and 12s.
The dog pants. I am in the van.
Ok.
Ok.

At a pet store I bought a soft-sided dog carrier. At the airport ticket counter my badge and employee ID. My blood distributed wrong. Uneven. Too much in my palms. Chest. Nothing in my toes. I will fly stand-by. Yes. I nodded. My destination and my credit card.

Every year we had two days of first aid and safety procedures. Before. When I was a stewardess. Flight Attendant. Recertification. "Annie, Annie. Are you okay?" and tests on what to do if the plane landed on the ocean. Every year the same filmstrip. The projector clicked. A whole hour. Various bad things. Plane depressurizes unexpectedly. Passengers riot. A man chokes on a peanut. The stewardess's calm, specific actions based in a firm understanding of protocol.

I no longer believe anyone would behave like they did in the movie. Demure. Returning to seats. Living. Mostly people might just go ahead and die.

There is no training video for this job, returning bags.

From the Baggage Redistribution Manual, xeroxed pages skewered into a 3-ring binder:

- *Customers are responsible for initiation of all communication.*
- *Customers may not handle the bag until it has been signed for.*
- *Carrier does not assume liability for customary wear and tear.*

I tell people, "It is protocol," and they listen.

For every question or problem, I have the answer. I can limit and direct every interaction.

Flight staff made me gate check the suitcase and cardboard box.

I didn't call Ray but I imagined sending him texts about duty and perseverance but those were not really the correct words and, also, he might tell me not to go.

I didn't call Mom. I would not have to until I was in Florida because she has agreed to not contacting the police until eight at night. A cruel thing I demand.

The flight attendant said, "Hello," at the mouth of the airplane.

"I am a trained stewardess. Let me know if you need any help," I said. Then I asked for seven little bottles of gin.

Middle seat. Middle of the plane. Over the wing. I stuffed Chantilly under the seat in front of me.

> August 22 (Later. Plane.)
> I am really trying. Let it in, FEAR. Embrace. Bumpy. Bumpy. Bumpy. I breathe the words. Redirect my thoughts away from the burning carpet. Necks broken. Redirect.
> The boy next to me. Arms across both armrests. I can only grip the seat cushion. And the pen. Toes forward to touch Chantilly's soft cage.
> I write. I write so that I can cling to the pen.
> He is asleep. The boy.
> I hate him.
> His calm.
> Now his arm shifts. Touches mine.
> Quiet.
> Oh.
> Take off.
> I am drunk.
> Ok.

> August 22 (Later. Plane. Still. At the gate.)
> Here. Listen.

The plane did not crash.
Bounce on the landing strip. The young man awake. Tilts his head. Says Home.
Ok.
Good-bye.

The baggage arrived. Plopped first off the incoming ramp, down and circled around on the metal conveyor. Drifted away, receded on the bowed slabs of metal that fold into each other at the corners. And then reappeared, chugging towards me. And away again. Eventually I picked them up, the brown fabric suitcase, the office supply box.

The air in the rented car. The taste of cigarettes and air freshener and my head spun more. I thought about keeping Chantilly in her carrier, but her panting coming from inside was terrible.

August 22 (Later. Car at airport.)
Mom sniffs at me when I get back from The Hills.
She comes out of the kitchen. Her plate of apples and peanut butter.
You are no daughter of mine when they haul you in drunk she says.
I do not want your apples anyway.
Ok.
Good-bye.
Also. After the divorce.
There was no question but that I could move back.
I live rent free.
Ok. Ok.
Good-bye.

I unzipped the carrier and Chantilly struggled out. Lowered her back end and looked at me. Shat on the passenger seat. I put the car in gear and drove. Ignored how she stared at me. Eventually I pulled over and scraped the poop out with the car rental receipt. Such a bad smell.

I dragged her into the rear seat. Too old to try to crawl forward. She whined.

"Why don't you go ahead and piddle on the seat?" I said. "Won't bother me."

She stopped whining loudly but a hiss, a soft cry, under each pant.

Swamp spilled out on both sides of the highway and we turned and turned until the road was a single-lane strip of blacktop with green shoots growing up through cracks. Only the occasional clapboard shack off in the distance, paint peeling, grey clothing heavy on the lines.

Before I saw the address I knew we had arrived. A mile away a wall up out of the swamp grasses. Hot pink stucco.

I parked on the gravel driveway. The gate. Smooth steel. Nine feet tall. Heat reflected off it and when I tipped my head I could see a shingled roof with multiple peaks beyond the wall. To the side of the gate a white doorbell button embedded into the stucco. I pushed it. Again. Again. Again. A piece of paper on the ground. A line of plastic tape, no longer sticky, fluttered at the top.

> *I will apologize for the inconvenience. However, nothing can change the truth that the doorbell will not signal your arrival. Please find your way inside and be announced at the entrance door.*

Signed Ms. Bilgue.

I pushed on the gate and it did not move. I burned the palm of my hand on the sun-hot metal and then set off to circle the fence. When I looked back Chantilly cowered against the seat back, trying to get out of the sun magnified through the windshield. I opened the door. She whined in joy. I picked her up and she peed down the front of my shirt. I said mean things and felt her small body covered in the matted fur shaking in my arms.

"Stupid dog," I said and locked the doors. I checked the trunk. Cross check complete.

I stumbled, clutching Chantilly, through the course grass that cut my legs. My shoes got soggy and the wall was three feet taller than my head the whole way around and no trees grew on the outside or reached over from the inside.

August 22 (Later. In the car. At the wall. Florida.)

I've stopped feeling much.

When the luggage arrived in Florida. Plop. First off the belt.

I am touching the space that is always worry.

Now it is. Unavoidable. Something about inevitable.

And exhaustion.

I touch that now. In me. Like I have melted. Just stay here blinking.

Whatever will happen will. I have felt that now. Since the airport. Have always suspected. Hoped. That my choices didn't matter.

I know that to be true now.

I used to root through the bags. When I first started. Peel back layers of underwear. Dirty. Clean. Toiletries. Shoes. Searching. Searching. All I ever found. Underwear and shoes.

Try to remember that.

Ok.

Good-bye.

I got in the car, Chantilly on my lap, and turned it on. I pressed the gas and considered ramming the vehicle into the hot pink stucco, in the middle, where the wall would be weakest. I did not because of the idea of Chantilly out there by herself if the wall didn't crumble and I died from the impact.

I pulled the car alongside the wall on the side with a bit of shade and rolled down the windows. I got out and popped the trunk. Mrs. Stiffton didn't appear. Standing on the roof of the car I could look over the fence. The house rose uneven and ramshackle, covered in long rows of faded blue shingles, round-bottomed, like teeth. A porch ran low to the ground along the front and circular windows that did not reflect the sun looked out from underneath the many eves. The brown suitcase landed lightly, right side up, on the other side of the wall, but the office supply box rocked up and flipped over and I heard the tinkle and shake of breaking glass. I pulled with my arms and scrabbled my feet along the abrasive stucco, trying to find traction and I pictured my rear end up in the air and I slid over the wall. I lay in the grass for a while, next to the suitcase and the box, looking at my palms that had turned pink from the paint.

"Bumpy," I said. "Bumpy, bumpy, bumpy." I did not start to panic and I did not know what to do with the absence of fear so I did some breathing anyway. In. Hold. Out. Hold. In.

Nothing happened when I knocked. I reached for the knob and pushed open the front door.

I yelled, "Hello," and shoved the box and the suitcase over the doorstop. I walked beyond the entryway and the house opened into a parlor with dusty pink and orange chairs lining the walls. Behind me a floorboard squeaked. Mrs. Stiffton darted around the corner, towards the box and suitcase.

She said, "Thank you for the delivery. Mrs. Bilgue regrets…"

I stepped towards her and I punched her. Hard.

She sat down on the ground and said, "Oh."

I said, "No. You can't have it. Mrs. Bilgue must present her ID and proof of flight and sign for the baggage. That is protocol."

"Well," Mrs. Stiffton stood up. "That will not be possible."

I punched her again. She sat down.

"I cannot accept anything else."

Mrs. Stiffton started to cry. She did not weep or really even have tears, but when she spoke again her voice came out rough and choked.

"You have to…"

"No," I said.

"Please," she said. "Please give me the bags. I have to get them. Please."

Down on the floor she was a small woman, her pants and shirt ballooning out from her belt, her stiff grey hair thin enough to expose the pale of her scalp. She looked up at me and her face seemed fragile and caught in shadow. Incomplete.

"No. Where is Ms. Bilgue and her identification?"

"You smell of urine." She did not say this cruelly, but sounded sad. "Wait." She stood up off the floor and went to the parlor. I began to scoot the baggage back to the front door.

"Here," she said. She held up *FEAR: Full Embrace Anxiety Response: embracing the emotions within.*

I said, "Jesus."

Then I said, "It's just old clothes and a toothbrush in that one. I looked. Whatever's in the box broke."

"Oh dear."

"Open the gate," I said.

"I can't," she said.

"How did you get in?"

She watched her finger as it touched a strip of wallpaper that had begun to lift away from the house. I saw humiliation in the hunching of her shoulders. I found I hoped she didn't know I saw her this way.

"Did it help? The book?" I asked.

"I don't know yet. You?"

"I haven't finished it."

I left the bags and I came over the fence, boosted on Mrs. Stiffton's knee and then cupped hands and then shoulder. On the top of the wall I lay flat for a moment, the stucco poking up into my stomach and cheek and my arms where I held the wall. I slipped down onto the car roof.

In the driver's seat I took several breaths. They felt good, not necessary.

"Bumpy," I said. Chantilly's tongue fell out of her mouth.

"Yes," I told her. "I still don't like that either."

I leaned down and smelled her sour fur.

I said, "Home."

AND WITH SUCH GREAT EFFORT TO ACHIEVE

Such a curious place...So strange a place. So unmagical. And with such great effort to achieve the unmagical. Bless them.

—Leonard Cohen, Live at Caesars Palace Coliseum, Las Vegas

Tari Ann Merrin loved Las Vegas. She did not love Las Vegas the way most people do, as a weekend spectator, a passive member of the desperate, debauched carnival. She loved all of Las Vegas, end to expanding end, desert to shrinking desert, mountain to mountain, and she loved it as blurry, black-and-white photos of a gasping train depot, a stop at a spring house along the road to California and she loved it in sepia and Technicolor and HD. She loved its 1950's homesteads and modern suburban sprawl and fourth-generation high-rise casinos. But most she loved it into the future. Because that is where Las Vegas really lives, in the dream of what it will be.

From the age of seven she knew that her life path lay in development and demanded to be taken out to see the bulldozers and cranes chewing at the land, erecting desert-colored houses. She stole flags that demarcated coming sewer and electric lines, mounted them on her walls like pennants. Through high school she worked for a grounds-keeping company that serviced homeowners' associations. Sometimes she filed paperwork and billed clients. Sometimes she spent after-school hours and long, hot summer days scattering gravel in yards and plucking thorns from the fat pads of decorative walkway cacti. She found these actions felt like devotional practice—prayer, and the kneeling and standing that comes with prayer.

She met Brad in Bar Green Mix Canary. His skin was evenly tanned and his features well arranged.

He said he worked at a country club and was training to be a professional golfer. He also toyed with high-stakes poker and day trading.

She said she worked at Caspian Lakes.

"Oh, Sweetie. I'm thinking about getting a place out there. Maybe you can talk to your boss and get me a deal?"

Tari Ann watched the dance floor and guessed which women were working and which were just there to have a good time.

"Or maybe I can buy you a drink," said Brad.

"Yes," she said. She drank it and then, with a pen that had Caspian Lakes Marketing and Construction, LLC inscribed up the shaft, sketched a map of the community on a napkin.

"Lots are available here." She made quick circles on the layers of thin paper spread between her fingers. "For you, I'd suggest the six-bedroom with the recessed front. Very popular."

She handed him a business card.

"CFOO. Wow," said Brad.

"This street here has yet to be named. Any suggestions?" She often asked buyers this.

He glanced again at her card.

"Tari Ann Street. That's what I'll vote for," he smiled, his teeth bleached and the tilt of his head practiced. "But you deserve an avenue."

"Keep the pen," she said.

Tari had come of age at the crescendo of the boom, when Las Vegas transitioned from a few houses surrounding entertainment strips to the national epicenter of the house-flipping game, 1.5 million people buying and selling, five-thousand residents in and three thousand out each month, the entire city buzzing like the floor of a stock exchange.

Tourism and cards, while integral to Las Vegas, were not, she knew, the future. Real estate, the purchase and sale of land and structure, that was the heart of the gamble.

"Even here, people want to be able to touch the things they have," she had told her college advisor. She skipped Hotel Management and Gaming Studies and got herself a MBA with a specialization in New Venture Management.

Brad purchased.

Construction would begin the next week.

They had drinks and dinner.

He called again. They golfed. He was very good.

Brad said, "Have you considered New York?"

Tari looked out over the fairway. Transplant, she thought. Transplanted citizens populated most of the city. The next move, where to go when their bank accounts bulged, how to get out, remained a key topic of conversation for these transplants. Tari knew that, in her native city, home ownership did not indicate home.

"New York lacks possibility," she said.

Tari Ann lived up near Celine Dion, at the western edge of Las Vegas's zoned land. She chose to not weigh in on the debate about building into the protected areas directly west of her doorstep, not the right moment in her career to take on either the Bureau of Land Management or the Vegas citizenry. She could not, however, drive past the flat desert rising up into the tremendous red boulder mountains without imagining multi-million-dollar homes speckling the land, a few cresting over the top of the bare hills. She would show these fresh, new houses at dusk, the rocks glowing pink and orange in the last of the sun, the city emerging below as an island of lights.

Besides the four-bedroom near Celine, she owned a condo far south on Las Vegas Boulevard, above the H&M in the Town Center outdoor mall. When tourists did not rent it off Craigslist she spent the weekend there. She partied at the mall bars, rose in the morning to jog the labyrinth of stores, touching the steps of the IMAX Cinema before turning to make her way back through the quiet, squinting against the harsh morning sun reflected out of plate-glass shop windows.

Under Tari's direction the planned community of Caspian Lakes had begun to inflate up out of the desert eleven miles east of the city, on the border of the Lake Mead National Recreation Area.

Caspian Lakes' high-end, pre-fab houses clotted the cul-du-sacs that trickled from a central ring road. The ring road circled Caspian Lake, a backhoed pit filled with water borrowed from Lake Mead, itself a bi-product of taming the mighty Colorado River with the Hoover Dam. Her contractors, replaceable and, thus, efficient, threw up buildings in a few days.

In an average week she and her team sold six to ten Caspian Lakes residences and she felt the community digging its hooks into the desert. Most people bought as a second, third or fifth home. To this majority clientele Tari referred to the cluster of houses as an *oasis*, conjuring ideas of travel and rest. To young people looking at Caspian Lakes for permanent residency, she spoke of *fresh starts*, a school that they could be instrumental in designing, safety and the natural environment: the lake, the mountains. For retirees, Tari Ann described fall concerts, the band floating out on the lake, cool breezes. "We have a water show here every week. The lake is equipped with fountains and we use the same designer as the Bellagio. Dancing Waters right here in your front yard." She also said *multi-generational* and *exclusive*. The floor managers at Caspian Lakes Casino told her which slots were loose and Tari Ann took interested buyers into the faux-hardwood and velvet parlor, sat them down and made sure they had enough free plays to come out ahead of the nothing they put in.

Tari Ann's team sold so well not just because they used the right words, offered their clients champagne and free money, but also because Tari loved Caspian Lakes and instilled this love in her employees.

She loved this satellite of Las Vegas erected out on the martian desert, Vegas extended as far as the BLM would allow. She was happy to gaze out at the lake, a dream realized, a lake made of a lake made of a river through the ingenuity of humans. She loved her carefully designed downtown street lined in dimly lit, cast-iron lamps and the two parks where families and lovers lay on manicured Astroturf and children played under industrial-sized sunshades angled against each other like sails. Sometimes when summer windstorms came out of the desert she imagined the buildings and the awnings catching that wind, lifting up and floating away, the Nina or the Pinta or the Santa Maria, off to find new lands to claim in the name of Las Vegas.

She continued to answer Brad's calls but she did not think about him when he wasn't there and she did not sleep with him until he showed her the bill of sale demonstrating that he had sold for a 50 percent markup.

"In only three weeks," she said. Her voice had gone husky. "Lots still available." She took off all her clothes and opened her legs.

"Who bought?" she said in his ear while they thrust together.

"A lonely, loaded, old couple from Lincoln, Nebraska. I want another one."

"A few left. Prices are up. You can have one if you can get the financing." She bit his shoulder. He smacked her ass.

Brad arrived at her office, a model home at the entrance to Caspian Lakes, in a polo shirt and khakis. Tari Ann did not kiss him and sent him out to the golf cart with another agent.

"I thought you would show me," he said.

"That is not really appropriate, is it?" she said. "We can have lunch after your tour if you like."

In the Bistro Barn, one of Caspian Lakes' premiere dining experiences, they ate tapas from a steel table.

"I should play it cool, but I love the lot," said Brad.

"You'll have great parties," said Tari Ann.

"I thought it might be a nice place for a family." He tilted his head and tapped his fork on the edge of his plate. "All the neighbors look married with kids."

She pursed her lips and looked away. "Parties."

"Parties," he said.

She said nothing. Vegas, while known for its easy divorces, married young. Most of the people she knew from high school lived with their kids and construction worker husbands and had paid for their weddings with tips from cocktailing and dealing lingerie blackjack. Tari Ann had too much to do to get married. She did not need to get married. She had Las Vegas.

Brad tapped his plate again.

"Why is it called Caspian Lakes? Will there be another lake?"

"Sounds better. Between you and me, it's the last lot. I'd jump on it."

"Isn't it a sea, anyway?"

"Fresh water."

The next time Brad called she intended to not pick up. But he didn't call and then the bubble she had constructed her life on burst. The housing market tumbled. A national and then international recession hit. The bulldozers and nail-guns grew silent outside the Caspian Lakes office. She smiled and talked about how there was nowhere to go but up. A hiccup, that's all. Can't keep Vegas down.

When he did call he had become unspecific in her memory. Her cell phone sat on up on a stack of books on her bedside table: *Igniting the Fire of Future*, *47 More Irrefutable Laws of Leadership* and *This Isn't Going to Work Out: Ending Employer/Employee Relationships*.

"My house is finished. I guess you know that. Can I give you a tour?"

She felt giddy as she drove from the management office to his house. A celebration. A home finished, not a house abandoned.

He had a bottle of gin waiting. She brought a box of condoms.

"The economy," he said.

"It will be fine," she said.

"Gas prices."

"Can't keep Vegas down."

"My buddies are thinking about selling."

"Look at that view. The Vegas Valley."

The market did not improve. In the mornings she read the short-sale notices as if they were obituaries and sometimes she moaned and sometimes she screamed and every day she felt her body smashing down a tall mountain, ledge after ledge. Every morning she went to work in fresh suits and perfect make-up.

Caspian Lakes emptied. In her upstairs office, what would have been the master bedroom with en suite bath, a Styrofoam-backed real estate map of Caspian Lakes lay spread out on a table. The map had once been a mosaic of green, yellow and blue flags—lots sold, lots with homes under construction, lots with complete houses and full or part-time residence. Now swaths of orange, homes abandoned to banks, waved up from the table.

The casino shut. SUV loads of the elderly arrived and circled the building, knocking on doors and peering in the tinted windows until they found the small "closed" sign and went away in confusion. Most of the boutiques pulled out, but Amber at the Wine Shoppe stayed afloat. She remained as the sole employee, twelve hours a day, selling cheap cabernet to the financially strained and several-hundred-dollar malbec to the unaffected while calculating the cost of keeping her stock at a healthy temperature. Friday night concerts persisted but hardly anyone drove around Caspian Lakes Rd. the rest of the week.

She saw Brad on Sundays for drinks or golf.

"We could just have sex," she told him.

They perched up on abnormally high stools, the tables supported on long, spindly legs. He looked around the murky bar, lighted mostly by covered candles, for a waitress. The waitresses wore black and Tari could only see them when the exposed skin of their arms or thighs reflected a small flame, like a mirror catching moonlight.

He hooked his finger in the air and thrust his chin up to catch the attention of a waitress. Then he took out an envelope and slid it across the table.

"It's a spa pass."

"Brad."

"A woman I give lessons to is friends with the owner." The waitress arrived and he ordered another drink, flirting in a way that Tari recognized as unconscious, the smile, the wink, but it still annoyed her.

"I could get another pass, if you want, for a girlfriend. Or they have this couple's thing," he told her.

"Oh."

When she didn't say anything else he said, "Well, anyway, she's a sweetie, this woman, but her stroke is terrible." He held his arms in front of his chest and tweaked his sleeves straight. "I'm giving up the Caspian Lakes house."

"Excuse me," said Tari. She stepped down off the high stool and walked away from the tall table. In the bathroom she locked a stall door and cried a little. Then she took a pen out of her clutch and wrote *the housing market made me consider him* on the plastic coating the metal wall.

The ink from the ballpoint pen came out in uneven lines so the message was legible only to Tari.

He loves me and the housing market makes me have a headache.

The message read *H l v me   d   h   .*

She tried to scratch out the letters but no ink flowed out. She kicked the wall and threw the pen in the toilet. The force of the flushing water was not strong enough to wash it away. She kicked the toilet.

At the table a fresh drink waited for her.

"Abandonment?" she said.

"It doesn't affect you, anyway. It's me and my credit report."

"It affects the value of other properties. There is a promise in a purchase. It affects…Las Vegas," she said.

"Don't use the word 'promise.' Jesus. I'm finished with my drink. You?"

Amber from the Wine Shoppe stopped by the office.

"I'm cutting my hours. Can't do it. Closing at six."

"Six," said Tari.

"It's just not worth it."

Tari Ann drove to Lake Mead and walked beyond what had been Echo Bay Beach to the lake's edge, down the long strip of gravel, past a few scrub bushes, where the water had drained away into people's showers and lawns. She squatted down and looked across the lake at the thick ring of mineral deposit marking the original water levels, now so far above the waves. Tari Ann felt thirsty. She felt alone.

"The war is lost," Tari said. "No, the war has moved on." She swept the Caspian Lakes Residencies map off the table. "Would you like to get naked?"

Brad unbuttoned his shirt and she pulled off her dress. She kissed his shaved chest and then pushed against it to make him lie on the table.

"Jacket," he said. She retrieved a condom from the pocket while Brad got out of his pants. She put her knee on the tabletop and hoisted herself up, his hands lifting and steadying her hips. He lay down again and she put his penis in her mouth, inattentively sucking and licking, until he was hard. She opened the condom.

"Are you ready?" he said.

She rolled it on and straddled him, sinking down, guiding him inside. She ignored the maple laminate grinding her kneecaps.

When they finished she remained astride him for a moment, contracting the muscles in her pelvis until he shrank and slipped out. She rose up, still on her knees and then climbed off the table. The tiny wood pins that had held the orange flags aloft on the map sunk into the carpet and the flesh of her feet. Tari bent one knee, looked over her shoulder and brushed the wood and plastic from her foot and then did the same with her other leg.

"I'm going to Mexico," she said. "I've done some research."

She went to take a shower. Brad knocked on the sliding glass door. She leaned back, the water pouring through her hair, sounding like wind as it hissed out of the fixture and hit the tile. Brad knocked again and she grabbed the thin metal bar affixed to the door, gliding it open a little.

They showered in silence, moving around each other, in and out of the water and then toweled off and dressed.

He stood behind her while she applied mascara.

"But, Las Vegas," he said.

"Moving on." She popped the brush back into its tube and screwed it shut with two quick twists.

The Costa Maya was almost full. Selling everything, her house, her condo, her shares, cashing in her retirement and talking to investors she knew, Tari financed a smallish piece of land with an eighth of a mile of beach, found a silent Mexican partner to sign the documents and got ready to build.

When questioned about her credentials she said, "Of course I can run a resort. I'm from Vegas. Besides, fifty percent of the units are set aside as condo purchase. It's going to be magic."

Hired men pulled out the trees, bared the earth and founded the first buildings. She fought the wet air, striding around the property, over the winding pathways outlined with ribbons of pink and yellow and red plastic supported by slivers of wood hammered into the ground. Visions of stucco walls, palm trees and sod, buffets and swim-up bars appeared before her. She drew in sharp breaths when she reached to touch a spiky palm frond or single-paned window and the mirage dissolved, leaving her in an expanse of lumpy dirt, cement foundations still cradled in wooden frames occasionally checkerboarding the brown soil.

"Faster," she said. "Let's do this thing. Vamos. We need some parrots."

The marketing team kicked around the name Lil' Vegas but decided that would not endear the resort to their target clientele: Non-Americans. Americans were out of money. They presented Tari Ann with a logo for Little Vegas instead.

"Little," she said. "Who ever wanted Vegas to be little?"

She fired them and informed the board of her actions in the same email as she proposed a new name: Mayan Vegas.

She wrote, "Here's a tag: *Why choose?* The economy is tough. Why choose? We offer individuals and families all the vacations they want—Las Vegas and the Mayan Riviera. I've had it translated into six languages, in case people like the idea."

People loved the idea.

Tari rented a short, single-wide trailer home and parked it near the beach. In the front end she had a computer, filing cabinets and a tiny table where she held meetings with the foreman and phone conversations with investors and architects. In the back a twin bed folded out of the wall, butting up against the stove, refrigerator and sink. She tried to take on the habit of siesta and, in the afternoon, lay on the bed listening to the grind of the generator. Inevitably, she remembered a phone call or email she needed to make or send and sat up, reached to the front and back of the trailer, got her phone or leaned her forearms on the table to type and, after a few minutes, abandoned the siesta. Outside she could see workers sitting in the shade of their trucks, eating huge meals out of coolers and playing dominos. She wanted to scream at them. *Stop looking so comfortable. I've only got a few months to build Las Vegas.*

In the evenings construction stopped with the sun. As the swollen clouds on the horizon fell dark, the men drove off in pickups or walked to the road to catch the bus.

She found it difficult to remember the names of the workers, Marco, Mario, Michael, Manuel. *Las Vegas*, they said, the *s*'s trickling out in slow, lazy rivers and the v settling somewhere close to b. *Nevada* they said with both *a*'s soft, low hills instead of pronouncing the first a as a sharp fall from a cliff, the way true Nevadans knew how. They said *Mexico* with a he in the middle that made the word a laugh, familiar.

The humidity gave her a rash. Her skin broke out as if she were thirteen.

She wore her makeup thick to cover the chaffed skin on her neck and the zits on her face. Streams of sweat streaked the makeup down onto her suit collars.

She could not go to her parents' house for dinner every two weeks. She could not say she remembered when the Mayan Riviera had been nothing but a few palapas shading hitchhiking hippies. Occasionally she drove her leased SUV up to the Ocean Mar Yucatan Resort and had a drink with the managers. They wanted to discuss home and the differences between home and Mexico.

She said, "Do you find the time-share more profitable than outright condo sale?" Or, "I'm thinking llama-drawn carts for the Mayan wedding packages."

She looked over the umbrellas and fruit skewers spiking out of her drink and forced smiles.

The managers went to get new drinks and did not return. She stayed at the table, shifting, shifting the coasters and napkins to mimic a perfect resort layout until the imperfectible design set her teeth on edge.

A few times she picked up guys from the schools of wrist banded tourists meandering through the Ocean Mar's Mayan Market Bar & Gift Shop and took them back to their rooms or to plastic-strapped chaise lounges on shadowed pool-sides.

Mostly at night she stayed in her trailer, an armed guard walking the premises, the screams of the parrots terrifying. She worked through the evenings, emails, budgets, Mayan Vegas emerging from the pressure of her fingers on the keyboard. She sent the board progress reports, *We are on target!* highlighting achievement and indicating entities that had tried to screw her over. *We are glad you're there,* wrote the board. *This is the level of expertise we had hoped for.*

Sometimes her concentration broke and she became aware of other things, the constant crash of waves, the almost imperceptible grit of sand rolling between the sheets and her legs.

The night the men finished the first building, twenty rooms, five with a pool view, she emailed photos to the new PR consultant, sat cross-legged in her rumpled sheets and mashed headphones into her ears. Conversación viente y ocho: Raúl pregunta direcciones a la tienda de ropa. Tari said, *cuadra, izquierda, norte, camiso,* and then yanked on the headphone cord. The tiny speakers pulled out of her ears and she heard silence, her windows shut, the air conditioner paused. She listened for the sound of the armed guard walking by. She thought his name was Eduardo or Hector and she felt how small and flimsy the trailer was, tin and vinyl and pressboard. She took out a tube of concealer and flopped the sponge across her face. She opened her screen door and yelled, "Hey."

"Hey," she yelled again.

Across the dark she saw the glowing end of the guard's cigarette.

"Hey."

She went out to him and knelt, ran her hands against the ground, until she felt leaves brush her palm.

"Here," she said. "Here," and pulled up the plant. "See?" She showed it to the man.

His body was thick and squat and he had a semi-automatic rifle strapped across his chest.

"Here," she said. "Come down here. You don't do anything all night." Tari pulled up the delicate leaves of another small plant. "These are weeds. We must stop them."

The man stepped back from her.

"Jesus Christ," Tari said and went back to her trailer, shutting the door tight against the night and the plants creaking up out of the earth.

The doctor in Cozumel spoke some English. He had her defecate into a tiny petri-dish.

"You have parasites," he said.

About the flakey white skin around the edges of her mouth he said, "Fungus. No make-up."

Tari Ann emailed Brad.

"I was thinking about that golf-course idea. Would you be interested in coming down to teach? I need someone with your talent and personality."
The board president visited three days before Mayan Vegas expected its first paying customers. Construction still raged and troops of maids walked across the pitted earth in their sturdy, low-heeled slip-ons, learning about bed making and vacuuming from their bilingual manager, in half-finished rooms and on mattresses stacked in suffocating impermanent metal storage units. The chef and his staff practiced the buffet—breakfast, brunch, lunch, dinner—feeding the workers. Tari Ann's stomach bloated.

She put concealer on her splotchy face and went out to meet the car. She hustled the president through the still unpainted entrance building.

"The Mayan Strip," she said, sweeping her arm out in front of her.

They walked up the three-acer path serpentining through shrunken Las Vegas attractions. A twenty-foot-tall Stratosphere, etched with Mayan glyphs, doubled as a climbing wall. New New York New York had a few feet of roller coaster track laid in a ring around it. Farther up a small gondola floated in a small pool. A man with a pole and in a Mariachi outfit stood at the helm.

"Get in. Get in," said Tari.

She pushed the president up the two steps and he awkwardly lowered himself into the rocking boat. Tari flipped a switch and a motor started up, making a current that the mariachi man used his pole to fight. The man sang "Guantanamera" over the sound of the motor, the gondola bumping the side of the pool.

"Oh. Yes," said the president, unsure where to look. When the man started in on the *ay ay ay ay*'s of "Canta y No Llores", the president said, "That was nice," and fled the boat.

They paused in front of the mini-MGM, what appeared to be an empty zoo exhibit.

"I'm glad you are here," said Tari. "The lion has been a problem with customs. What about using a person? Kind of a Cirque thing. Cheaper. Or iguanas. Think about it. Let's show you your room."

She took out her concealer.

Tari Ann believed in Mayan Vegas. She believed in the design, each small building a Vegas experience made intimate. A few go-go dancers in Caesar's Casa, three blackjack tables at the Mandalay Bahía, Paco Suza Ilusíonista, family friendly from noon to eight, adult themed from eight to one, performed atop the indoor Eiffel Tower at Parisíto and video poker machines in each building. Labor was inexpensive enough to have someone at every door who could say, *Sorry, we are full. You will enjoy El Grupo de Hombres Rojo at the Treasure Cay.*

Watching this American in his Hugo Boss pinstripes she felt, for the first time, that the buildings might be small, not intimate, that a climb on her Stratosphere could not compete with the huge walls up the coast at Club Med or a bungee jump off the real building.

She found a foreman and told him, "You. All of you need to know that to have a return you must invest. I am watching." She tapped the side of her head, near her eye.

Brad arrived. His tan was perfect and his shoulders broad. Tari Ann rubbed on more concealer. She took him to his room and shut the door, but the sound of hammering and electric saws still came in.

"Vegas cannot question itself," she said.

He put his hands on her hips.

"I don't think I can," she said and tried to suck in her ballooned stomach.

Brad pulled out some papers covered in elaborate script.

"It's a gift. A deed. For a piece of the moon," he said.

"I don't have a space ship."

He walked to the window and touched the frame.

"Is this legally binding?" she asked. "Tari Ann? What's that?"

"On the far side. A crater. It seemed more right than a sea. Look on the satellite photo. Next to Izcak."

"We can't build on the moon yet. I'll show you the golf area."

There was a putting green and a small corridor of driving range.

"No course," said Brad.

"We've got a lot to do. Our funding. All those trees. They aren't even mine. I've got a conference call. The chef will make you whatever you like but say it in Spanish."

She smeared concealer on her face.

She could feel Brad staring after her and did not breath until she heard his club swish through the air, crack against balls.

In the first week tourists trickled in. They came for the grand opening deals, Germans and Italians wading through the pools. They hunched over video poker machines and took meringue lessons on the beach. There were not many of them, not the drunken herds in Speedos, shelling out for the sightseeing tours and the taxies that promised kickbacks to Mayan Vegas, not what Tari Ann had expected and she sent staff to the Cancun airport to clack together coupons for free shows and drinks in the faces of tourists waiting to be put in vans and whisked to other resorts.

"Like this." She wrenched the wrists of her employees. "Like this. They have got to go click click. Want it. I'll know if you don't. Say it: Our all-inclusive can include you."

Brad taught a few lessons. Private or couples. The area was not big enough for anything else.

She had her trailer pulled into the jungle skirting the resort and lay there at night, her stomach cramped, till she rose to hunt weeds.

By the end of the first week Tari had sold none of the rooms as vacation condos. The authorities had come three times and extracted huge cash bribes to keep quiet about the blackjack tables. The gondola leaked from smashing against the pool wall and the Stratosphere had a crack running down the middle of the poured cement.

"We'll put some steel cable around it. It's fine. Tie pillows to the boat. Call it a dream boat."

It was noon. Brad sat at a row of video poker machines in the dark of Caesar's Casa. No tourists came in and the go-go dancers lounged on the stage, chatting. Tari closed her eyes, angry that she could not remember how to say *stand up* in Spanish. At her hip a walkie-talkie crackled and she hoped someone would need her. Brad put a dollar in a machine.

"It accepts dollars," he said.

"And Euros."

"I'm not going to make it pro."

He tapped the computer screen.

"You know, you told me there would be a course here. I thought there was something I could be a part of. And that you might be asking me to come."

"I did."

"You asked a golf teacher. The money's better in Vegas."

"Vegas is dead," she said. "Vegas lives here now."

"Honey."

"*Honey* my ass."

"I've had an offer from a place in L.A. And they need a sales exec, too," he said. "You've had some setbacks."

"You don't see it. You've never seen it. You talked about New York, about L.A., the first time we met. You're like them all. The oldest living things in the world grow in the desert and in the mountains of Vegas. Bristlecone pines. Scrubby and hard as a rock and four thousand years old. Nothing grows like that here. Here I go to sleep and in the morning a tree has shot up outside my window. But those pyramids. All those Mayan pyramids, they got built and everyone was sacrificed on them and they were telling the calendar back when the bristlecone started. That desert? How can people stay there? Where it is so slow? Everyone goes. The Indians and the prospectors and the Mob, for God's sake. But here. Maria. Are you Mayan? Of course she is. You know how the desert smells in the rain. Creosote. Growing a centimeter a year. Spiky plants with tiny leaves, little nothing bushes five-hundred years old out next to a freeway. Out behind the Golden Nugget. Creosote are clonal. They grow in rings, a single plant sending branches farther and farther out. The center dies but that land inside, the water, the space for roots, the creosote claims it. There is a bush in the Mojave that is twelve thousand years old. And only so big. How can Vegas live in such a place? Those tortoises all wrinkled like old men and haven't done anything but sleep in their holes for twenty million years. Vegas can't be there. But people that understand don't forget all those slow, hard plants. How to not wait for paradise. Here. Here is the place. Here, where every morning the land is new."

She snatched out her concealer.

The walkie-talkie said, "Incoming."

She yanked it off her belt. "Roger."

She walked from the casino and outside a van opened its doors and four tourists, ooing and ahing the Mayan Strip, stepped out.

"Thank you," she said to the driver whose name was Rudolfo or Rodrigo. She bent to pull a weed and then turned to the visitors.

"Welcome," said Tari Ann. "Welcome to Mayan Vegas. If you have a dream we will make it come true."

ALL THE THINGS I KNOW

Dear,

I regret the gums and teeth. The new heart valves. I loathe my endlessly spry knees and firm muscle tone.

For a while I tried to get them to work on the problem. The rocks. Something must be done and we can't solve it so I outsourced to the rocks. Living here with them I've become sure they have brilliant ideas.

Still, I have heard nothing from the boulders or the cliffs. The pebbles are mute and that brings up the point about what makes me think that they would help, even if they could. What have we ever done for a rock? Far as I know we let them alone or smash them up. Cement and such. So what's in it for them?

That's not really my point. My point is they are rocks.

It is an issue of communication.

I cannot argue that they don't have tons and tons of time to speculate on the situation, though maybe they have their own concerns to prioritize, but I cannot interpret their expressions.

However, we are too far gone to make such claims on logic or knowledge.

I have heard nothing from them. I grow frustrated.

Without any new ideas from the rocks, this is what I know:

One. I'm done. No more, thank you.

Two. We humans, we are meant to live only so far.

Three. This is because one human can take only a limited amount of surprise and resignation to consequences.

Four. We humans never end now, replacing the body piece by piece. The consequence surprises us. We struggle to be resigned.

Five. My body, every morning, tick, tick, tick, up and at 'em. My mind as sharp or as dull as ever. The hormones kick and the electrons fire. But, referring to the first thing I know, I'm done. The warranty on the engine all used up.

Six. How short-sighted, humans. It gets us in trouble. I'm in that kind of trouble. The consequence of desire without forethought. Surprise! Try to be resigned.

Everything else is elaboration on the things I know.

I wish I only knew only five things because then I could keep all the things in one hand.

I do not know my age. I stopped caring. I moved to the desert where the days turn on and turn off with the rise and set of the harsh sun so that I would not have to watch time mock me with its notable daily shortening and then lengthening of shadow, with the everyday gentling of the evening light. I moved here where no seasons that suggest death could taunt me. I imagine that I am, each day, living the day before again. I work towards the perfect execution of a day: perfect exhaustion. I have a perfect tan.

All of us with our new bits and pieces, the liver, the elbow, cannot believe how we begged and begged to be allowed to stay. Now we want to sneak out before the party is over. Rude. Ungrateful. Shameful. Wasteful. All the plastic and technology. Our grudging existence, it's embarrassing and affects all of us poorly. The species. We, the remade and weary, are becoming rotten apples.

That is a painful expression I wish I had not used. We cannot rot, the plastics and metals, of course. But we drag, pull on the rest. We are becoming dead weight.

That was not a good choice either.

I will speak in specifics to avoid the accidental pain of metaphor. We, the remade, scoff at desire to live, at that verve the young have. We are jealous. We exude futility.

I know the caveman that burned up his family, sparks flying, as he piled and piled wood on the fire, desperate to see the largeness of its

possibility. I empathize with the man who shot his son up in the rocket, strapped him in, attempting to achieve orbit with the lighter body
weight, and did not raise his slow legs, encumbered with flesh and bone,
to run toward the rocket explosion on the horizon. I dream of rust.

I have become the keeper of this desert. I was alone. Now the remade come for renewal of their too-old beings. They stumble around
wanting to remember what anticipation feels like. A rumor started.
Someone whispered that the sand had scoured away the exhaustion
of age and that they bloomed with the cactus flowers, that they kicked
off their shoes and wiggled their toes, elated to see their body still
so supple. They did knee bends and sang and walked on their hands,
praising the smooth glide of their plasticed joints and the elastic
strength of their diaphragm.

I am still alone. They do not talk to me, those who come seeking.
They slip off over the rises of sand, they follow jack rabbit trails, remembering, or not remembering but making a memory, telling themselves of a childhood when a jack rabbit trail would have meant the
greatest day. They wave to Joshua trees far in the distance, walk out
to greet them. They imitate a human desire for quest.

I find their failure. Their parched lips, their wrists pricked a million
times with agave thorns. I find them still clutching the earth and jealous,
into the end, of the patience of rocks.

There is a sprinkler in front of my shack. I don't know why. One
sprinkler. I don't know where the control is, what turns it on and off.
A few times a day a perfect cone of water arcs up and drops down into
the dirt, a tutu glittering, hovering. Once I thought about a lost nymph
wandering in the desert. Then I remembered what a silly thing that
would be to think. After the sprinkler stops everything feels mundane.

When I find the remade out in the desert they do not look relieved.
They simply look finished. I have not had a perfect day yet. The day
I am not surprised or regretful of my consequences, then, maybe
then, I will go out and, I think, then I will sit amongst the jackrabbits
and Joshua trees and wait, patient, for my body of plastics and metals
to turn to rock. I will feel the exhaustion seep down, running to disappear, absorbed through the sand. I will know if the rocks regret,

if they sigh shame in eons of breath and rage and fear. They might tell me answers.

These are the things I do not want the next groundskeeper to see on my face: regret, shame, fear, anger. I am old enough to know better.

Yesterday evening someone came here and said he was my son.

I explained that we have gone beyond that. We no longer have child. Parent. The process of caring for and being cared for has ended.

He walked out into the desert night, his tread heavy, and today, when the sun turned on, I looked at the gouges his shoes made into the desert. I long to put my feet in those depressions. Start out after him. But what if I find him dead? What if I find him tending a bush, talking to it, caressing the air around its prickly leaves, spitting to moisten the soil that encases the roots? What if I find him anything except turned to rock?

THE PRINTED BABY

Still, caution remains important. The use of fetal ultrasound solely to create keepsakes isn't recommended.

—The Mayo Clinic

We printed her after we lost her. We printed her before we lost her, also. Two weeks before. Maybe a little more. Back when she would become something more, before the printings were all that she would be. Maybe a long time before. Look at me. I pretend like I don't remember the exact chronology. Sometimes I don't remember the chronology.

knowyourbaby.com says this week your baby is the size of a lemon. This week an avocado, a peach, a cactus fruit. This week. We first printed her, week eighteen, three-dimensional print, plastic, like icing, oozing out of the machine to mimic her arms and legs and body, when she was the size of a sweet potato, eighteen weeks. We had just found out it was a her. I remember laughing. Don't breathe the fumes, pregnant lady. Don't hurt her, pregnant lady. Now we have printed her three times. Week eight, size of a cranberry bean. Week eighteen, size of a sweet potato. Week twenty, size of an artichoke, one for each ultrasound.

Ultra.

The ultimate.

Jake did it without asking. Jake did the second printing without asking. Without talking to me about it, I don't know, sometime after she was only a printing, one printing, nothing more in my body. She was only a printing, week eighteen, size of a sweet potato and then he did the second printing, week eight, size of a cranberry bean, without asking. I came home and, as always, knew, as I knew all day and night, that she was, printed, smooth and cool and impervious, week eighteen, size of a sweet potato, living in the house, one arm forever raised towards her mouth. I touched the door of the room we had started to decorate for her. I don't believe I entered. Maybe I entered and thought about crooning animal noises. I found Jake down with the 3D printer and he turned and held her out, eight weeks, size of a cranberry bean. Before she was a she. Arms and legs all the same size.

"Kumquat," he said.

"Cranberry bean," I said.

She lives now in smooth, cool perfection. It would be hard to harm her. Things like germs or a great personal loss would change nothing.

Lives, in such cases, is a political word. I don't want to be political. I give money to Planned Parenthood. I have t-shirts and bumper stickers that support choice and I don't want to debate if she ever lived, what is lived. She existed. She exists now.

Size of a cranberry bean, eight weeks, she exists, arms and legs the same size. She is a lump of head and a lump of body. A toy bear but the word toy. I don't like it.

Size of a sweet potato, eighteen weeks, and size of an artichoke, twenty weeks, she is spindly old man legs and arms and mostly a head and she seems to want to bend but then, if you touch her, is hard. She is an alien from a 1950's B-movie. She is her first trip to the zoo. She is nothing. She is all the years of school photos. She has gone wrong.

This smooth baby does not betray what was inside the wet and lost baby. The flaw. The little wrongness that made her incapable of going on. Unviable.

I don't know what a cranberry bean is, week 8. I know it is very small because Jake printed her to scale and we have her now, cranberry bean, eight weeks. Perhaps she is not actually size of a cranberry bean, but size of a kumquat, week ten. "That website is really reaching for fruits to compare embryos to," Jake said the week of the kumquat, when she still was, before we printed her, before she was only a printing, we took to calling her, it, *Kumquat.* Because the word is vague and friendly and foreign sounding.

"Sing to me," I ask him. "Sing to me." I do not want him to speak and I do not want silence. What use is silence? He turns on music and I wonder if he could possibly think that pressing the button feels the same as singing.

My mother has her bronzed baby shoes. My grandmother has a pair of shoes, bronzed, that a baby never wore. When I was in high school I found them in a box in her attic.

"Are these Daniel's?" I asked, assuming they were my uncle's.

"Sarah's," Grandma said, a name I could not attach to any family member.

I mumbled, "Oh," embarrassed at my poor ancestral knowledge.

"Who's Sarah?" I asked my mom later.

"A sister," she said. Her eyes slid sideways, away from mine.

I had not yet had sex but, years before and maybe until I graduated junior high, I had, as children do, stuffed a pillow up my shirt, "I'm pregnant." And countless dolls. I had, playing in my room, birthed countless dolls. And stuffed animals.

We were so careful. We did not call her "baby." I did not think of her as "baby" until she was only a printing. Fetus. Always fetus, like the name of a disease, a Roman ruler. Latin and medical. Certainly not round and clean.

The printings. Where do they go? Where do they belong? In her room. Sometimes out on the couch with us. Once at the dinner table. I look at the printing, ears and knuckles, the color of spoiled butter, and tired breaks down the carefully maintained linguistic walls and I think, "Baby."

The first thing we printed was more parts for the printer. What delight to own a machine that could make itself. "We live in a sci-fi novel! A machine that can make itself," we giggled. "Let's make ourselves," we said and took off our clothes and made an embryo inside me while the machine slowly layered plastic to make a machine. Now I catch myself wondering why the machine won't turn on and make more parts of the baby. All the inside parts. Fix the design. Find the glitch. Or print new parts for the parts of me that made a broken baby.

She would not have lived if she had not died inside me. I try to find better words. Words that understand that even in the past there was never going to be a future. After she was, before we knew that she would not be, before she would be only eight weeks, size of a cranberry bean, size of an artichoke, size of a sweet potato, ethically I would have supported me in my own decision to end the pregnancy. But we wanted a kid, the poop and the first time she hated us and the bike riding and loving a kitten too rough. She was the next step. Correct. We embraced our biological drives.

"Well, honey," says my mom and the thought, "It was not meant to be," comes into my mind and I want to take a hammer to the head of our printed baby.

I did not know that the artichoke is considered larger than the sweet potato.

At the hospital they said, "No fetal heartbeat." Confirmation that she had stopped being. "I'm sorry, Mr. and Mrs. There is nothing we can do. You have some options for expelling the tissue." And a 3D ultrasound to take home.

Sometimes, after she was, before she was a printing, before she was only something unquestionable, sometimes we found knowyourbaby.com's fruit or vegetable of the week at the grocery store. The peach. The lime. The Brussels sprout. The blueberry. We bought a pound. Two pounds. "Feed the fetus," we said, and gobbled all the produce up. Now, always, the grocery store is full of sweet potatoes. They keep well. They grow them in Chile when you can't grow them here. They are not seasonal. I want to run from them. I want to buy them all so no one else can have them. I want to bury them, each one. I want to eat them all raw. Sometimes, though, I don't care about sweet potatoes. The sweet potatoes will never be anything but sweet potatoes. I can't remember what months are artichoke season, when they will suddenly feature in the produce section, spiky leaves reaching up, up, a baby on its back, hard, molded hands to the air.

The flaw could be in us. Between us. In us coming together to make a thing. We also chose a poor paint color for the living room. Too green. When I was a child I made two excellent pillows in Home Ec class. My mother still has them on her couch. Jake and I tried to construct a throw pillow and, together, we could not sew a right angle. Often when we walk we fall out of rhythm with each other and one of us must do a skip-step so that our feet can hit the ground at the same time again. I think of his preferred patterns on stoneware as completely wrong. I have all of this language. DNA. Genetic. Predisposed. Hereditary. I understand these words enough to use them as explanation of things I do not want to define with more basic language. A defense.

We printed her the third time, week 20, size of an artichoke, at some point. See how I pretend not to know exactly when we did the last printing. Nonchalant. Less invested. Here is when we did the third printing: at the moment Jake turned around from the machine and had her, eight weeks, size of a cranberry bean, before she was a her, legs and arms the same size, had her fresh printed in his hand. I touched her, eight weeks, size of a cranberry bean. Smooth. Tiny. Something you might lose down the back of the sofa. The fingers webbed and useless out in the thin air. Something not made to live in our house unless placed on a shelf and dusted annually. Now there on Jake's warm hand. Always warmer than mine. And her upstairs, week eighteen, size of a sweet potato, arm bent towards her mouth.

"Do it. Do the other one," I said.

"I don't know if we should,"

"Should?"

"Why?"

"Why?"

"It just seems…"

"I didn't choose about that," I pointed to the baby, size of a cranberry bean, in his hand. I picked it up, gentle, two fingers. I didn't like making the pinching motion, how you pick up small, unimportant things. I considered swallowing her but that felt obvious. Kissing her felt insincere. And screaming. I could not bathe her in tears and I looked at Jake, wild that he would see how I couldn't cry, wild that my lack of demonstration would undermine the seeming intensity of my want to print her again, week 20, size of an artichoke. I had not, previously, considered him much in the grief because we had not differed in our grief.

"I did not get to make a choice about this and you do not make a choice about the last one. Print the last one."

"In that one she is dead."

"Most of what I know about you is dead. Because it is not here anymore. It is over. I want everything of her."

I spat on her, size of a cranberry bean, and cleaned her gently with my shirt.

"Try again," says my mom over the phone.

I say nothing.

I sit on the floor. My upper back leans against the side of our bed. My lower back leans against nothing. My knees are raised and, week 18, size of a sweet potato, she lays on the carpet and against my hip.

After she was and before she was a printing Jake made a me a set of jewelry with the machine—rings, bracelet, tiara. A thing to squeeze the toothpaste tube flat and empty, which I said was passive aggressive because he likes to squeeze from the bottom and I don't care and often forget and squeeze in the middle. He did some sculpture pieces and was putting together a show. And all the babies for our friends. Sure, we said, send us your ultrasounds. We'll make you a baby. Ship them around the country. You never know when you are making not a memory but the memory.

I found Jake at the changing table that had arrived days before the abdominal pain started. I stood and he dressed her, eighteen weeks size of a sweet potato, in a onesie, snap at the neck, three down below. She did not cry. She was the plastic doll on who I learned CPR. She was our printed baby.

"More like a papaya," I said.

"Big for her age," he said.

I laughed because it seemed really funny.

She had a few strands of hair, bumps, strings of plastic, raised along her head.

"How long do we do this?" he said.

"Do what?" I said.

"How long do we do this?"

"Sing," I said.

"No," he said. "Not with you here."

"We do it until we don't."

"Go into the living room and I'll sing."

So I went and sat on the couch and his voice, "Are you sleeping, are you sleeping," came, muffled, into the room.

Mom sends recipes to us every week. She has done this my entire life and, when Jake and I married he began to get them also. One week, after we had only the printings and carried them, secrets, from room to room and told no one about our printed baby, she sent a recipe for artichoke dip. When it came into our inboxes, our phones chiming message alert together, Jake looked and laughed and I looked and laughed. I did not feel that it was funny but I knew it should have been so I laughed. Week 20, sized for an excellent dip.

If you go to the reduced version of the Oxford English Dictionary that is available on my phone and look up "give birth" you find this definition: "Bear a child or young." I can't help but enjoy the easy and profound ache of things like definitions.

I chose for them to give me a pill and I bled and bled and eventually, size of an artichoke, she slid out. We did not see her. We chose not to see her, blooded and not alive flesh.

"Did you get the recipe for the dip," says Mom.
    "Yes," I say.
    "Did you try it?"
    "Not yet."

"To bear" Carry. Display. Have as a physical mark or feature. Be called by (a name or title) conduct oneself in a particular manner. Support. Take responsibility for. Be able to accept or stand up to. Endure. Produce. Turn and proceed in a specific direction. Give birth to (a child.)

I bring her, week twenty, size of an artichoke, to Jake. The printings, she, have not found a place. In the morning and when I come home I seek them and carry them to new places. Jake finds them and carries them to new places. Both of us cats carrying kittens by the scruff, seeking a safe den.

"Sing to her."

He doesn't.

"Why?" I ask.

"Honey."

"Why?"

"It's the wrong one."

"Why?"

"Honey."

"Why?"

"The fetal heartbeat."

I know that these words, fetal heartbeat, that build a fence with blunt, distant, medical syllables are Jake being kind, gentle.

"Sing. Please," I say.

"I think we should try again. I mean. Statistically…"

And I am in the baby's room, half a forest painted on the wall, the babies, cold and smooth, gathered in my arms.

"Storage?" I ask. "Do we store her? She will not biodegrade."

Jake says nothing.

"I am not ready to have a different have," I say.

"Alright," says Jake and I think he will take all the babies from me and lay them quiet somewhere. Instead he turns and leaves me alone in the room and I know that I hoped that he would take them and that, if he had taken them I would have cried in rage at his action.

In the night I go into the changing table and, eighteen weeks, size of a sweet potato, and I unsnap the onesie. I take her out and whisper a repentance. I touch her and she has not become warm and she does not cry tears. In the darkness I had already found her size of a cranberry bean, size of an artichoke, in a chair, on a Kleenex in a bowl, elsewhere in the house, and she has not become flesh. I gather her together. I cuddle the hard, fixed baby to my chest. It is silly to imagine the changeling returned to her family and I imagine it every night. I think that maybe, the next time I open the door she will be remolded, remade. Perhaps a shoe. Perhaps a great giant stalk of plastic through the roof.

MARVELOUS

They met on a boat that soared and plummeted in tall gray waves.

Bent down in order to grip the ferry's railing, Devin felt more awkward than usual. To pass the time, and because of habit, he ran calculations in his mind, occasionally whispering to himself and only partially focused on the task. The boat headed towards an island just off the coast of Honduras and he estimated the distance increase he would experience due to the rise and fall of summiting the whitecaps instead of traveling a flat sea.

In a moment of calm he watched a woman, angular and with high cheekbones, come across the deck towards him.

"It's marvelous, isn't it?" Her accent was American. She gripped the railing as the boat rolled into the hollow of another wave. "Marvelous."

After five years in Honduras he found her English foreign-sounding, American, though he knew it must be like his own.

"I was raised around boats. I always miss them," she shouted over the water and the boat engine.

"Are you talking to me?" he asked.

"Yes. Of course. Does the sea make you sick?" She looked at him inquisitively but without concern.

"No."

"Good." Her eyes were grey and she wore the sort of thin cotton shirt common among backpacking travelers. It should have billowed around her but, wet from the waves, the fabric hugged tight against her bony body. She shivered, though her face did not acknowledge the cold. He wanted to wrap his arms around her.

The boat lurched. Water slapped their feet and a man beside them moaned. She pursed her lips at him in disapproval.

"I heard that at sunset iguanas and crabs take over the roads on the island," she shouted.

"In the back. Where people don't live."

"It's on my list."

He let the next rock of the boat shift him so his arm touched hers, just above the elbow. She did not move away.

Her name was Octavia and on the island they checked into the same little hotel.

They ate fish and rice and refried beans and drank Puerto Royal and shots of tequila. She insisted on the tequila in order to have something exotic and imported.

He told her, "Five years ago I bought a plane ticket to Tegucigalpa. I guess I liked the name. Needed a break. I didn't like it. Tegucigalpa. So I got on a bus out of the city and I saw this mountain covered in jungle out of the window. So I got off."

"You fell in love," she said.

"I fell."

"And where is she now?"

"Married with two children," he said. "With another man," he added. "This island was populated by British pirates once."

She whined with the bar owner to a string of Caribbean songs. Devin wouldn't dance. He calculated the average gyrations of her ass per hour.

When she sat down she leaned against him.

"Marvelous," she said.

In the morning they snorkeled. They ate shrimp. He didn't go see his friends on the island.

She was an artist and older than him and carried a folded piece of graph paper covered in tiny, scrunched handwriting in a plastic baggie.

"My list of things to do," she said.

"Let me see."

"No. Only me."

"Why?"

"I don't know. I do know. Should I tell you? It's that in case I don't do something only I will be disappointed. In myself."

At a white-sand beach they waded in the warm ocean and kissed under the waxing moon.

"It's a little ridiculous," she said, pinching his ear. "The moon and all."

They dried their feet on her sweater and walked until hundreds of moon-made shadows skittered off the road and rustled into the underbrush.

"Crabs in the moonlight. That's on the list." She took the paper out of the baggie and made a thick line through some of the words.

It seemed obvious that he should love her, so he did. They slept together on a lumpy hotel mattress.

After, she took out her list and added something to it.

He resisted asking what it was an instead said, "What's your favorite word?"

"Start," she said. "Maybe begin." Octavia dragged her finger down the center of his chest until it came to rest in the hollow of his navel. "Your bellybutton looks like a pouting child." She stuck out her lower lip. "What's yours?"

"Fly."

She buried her head between his arm and chest.

"I had these dreams when I was very young," said Devin. "I flew. I stopped having the dreams and so I tried swimming and diving. Space world. Nothing feels the same as the dreams. Effortless. It's about aer-odynamics…" he stopped himself.

"How wonderful to have something, one thing, to be passionate about. I've always wanted that."

"I'm working on a PhD. MIT. Physics. I was…I am interested in flight. Every semester I defer."

"Marvelous," she breathed.

"In Massachusetts I had these parakeets. One day I let them out to fly around the apartment. After a bit they went back in their cage and waited for me to shut the gate. God. Then I came here."

"I am careless with people's hearts, mine included," she told him.

When he left the island she came back across the water, calm on the return trip, to La Ceiba with him.

In his bed, comfortable and quiet, her head against his chest, he smoothed the heel of his hand over the fine wrinkles cresting across her forehead.

"I want to show you something," he said.

"Ok."

He pulled her up out of bed and wrapped her sarong around her body and put on his boxers.

"Close your eyes," he said and was amazed when she did and when she let him lead her, arm around her thin waist, pulling gently on her hand, through the concrete back patio and into his butterfly house.

Walled in netting and furnished with plants that grew out of the earth, the Butterfly House, La Casa de las Mariposas, was both cooler and more humid than the rest of La Ceiba. During visiting hours, brick paths guided tourists and affluent Hondurans through the leaves and blooms where hundreds of butterflies, over thirty species, ate and mated and died. A year and a half before the place had been a bare, broken slab of cement. Now the air sparkled with the wings of butterflies, iridescent green, red, orange and purple, as if a pillow stuffed with the feathers of jungle birds had been ripped open in a breeze.

His joy. La Casa de las Mariposas. The constant flit and float of the butterflies brought him closer to the sensation of flight than all the hang-gliding or skydiving he had done. He lifted one arm, taking a stance he imagined to be proud and welcoming and confident. A *Caligo brasiliensis*, with palm-sized, gray-white underwings patterned with owl eye camouflage, landed on his finger and he imagined himself a falconer who had whistled and caused the return of his fine-boned raptor. The butterfly sat with its wings spread open, a rare thing, showing off brilliant blue-green fibers, an unwrapped gift.

He looked down at Octavia, her eyes closed, gathering the orange sarong at her chest. Perfect, he thought. "Perfect," he whispered. "Ok. Open your eyes," he said to her.

For a moment her face was blank. The butterfly on Devin's finger lifted off, fluttered towards her and Octavia began to yell and rake at the delicate wings of the Brassolide.

"No," said Devin.

She screamed and swung at the air and fell to the ground. She curled up, hands covering her head, sarong opening to expose her thighs and breasts. He had to drag her from La Casa de las Mariposas.

Later, slouched on the couch with a cool bottle of Aguazul pressed against her left temple, she said, "I'm phobic."

"Yes," he said. "Always?"

"Well, usually just one flying...thing, it's ok. I can control it. The fear, I mean."

"Birds?"

"Birds are better. Bigger. But I don't do so well in parks. With the pigeons. They come so near." She closed her eyes.

"I didn't know."

"Yes. Of course. I didn't tell you."

"A surprise," he explained.

She shuddered.

"So that it would be a surprise," he said.

"Yes. And your dreams of flying. And the moon. It's so easy to ruin things like this so I didn't say anything."

Devin was quiet and then he said, "You will stay for a while?"

She ran her toes across the white tile floor.

"Octavia." He touched her hand.

She shrugged. "For a bit."

Every night for a week he woke to her screaming, flailing at the air around her head so that he had to hold her wrists to keep from being punched. After she was conscious she shook and sometimes cried as he rocked her and listened to the occasional night traffic. She knotted her hair up into a bun and tied scarves over it. She looked at photos of butterflies and moths and giant bumble bees but she did not get better. Constantly agitated, a breeze on her face or seeing a curtain shift out of the corner of her eye made her cringe, jerk her hand up to protect her head.

"I think I can't stay. I'm sorry. It's that that place is right there," she gestured towards the Casa.

"No. Please. Not yet. Give me a week."

He ripped up the jungle plants. He had solid walls of cinder block and plaster built. The bricks from the pathways were stacked in the patio and flooring was laid in their place. Before that he opened the doors and shooed the butterflies out. Before that he captured two males and two females of each species and ushered them into kill jars. Onto tiny cards he typed species names, M or F, dorsal or ventral, and the locations where he had captured their ancestors so many butterfly generations ago. He tacked each insect and its correct card to corkboard. When the walls were finished he hung the rectangular boards at exact intervals over the fresh paint.

He wept and wept and then dried his eyes and went to Octavia who wrapped her arms around him.

"Maybe you'll get your dreams back," she said.

"This is enough," he said.

They lived very well by Honduran standards, mostly unaffected by violence or politics. She was known as La Artista and he was known for his butterflies. Their life was quiet. When she could not stand the quiet she threw parties with cases and cases of Puerto Royal. She did charcoal sketches of the guests as party favors and Devin locked himself in La Casa until it was over. As the sudden dawn came up over the ocean he slid into bed, nuzzling against her neck and she wrapped her legs around him, caressing charcoal smudges from her fingers onto his cheeks and lips. He did not dream of flying but he helped secure money for national parks, trained guides in the specifics of Honduran entomology and translated tourist materials whenever anyone asked him to. Octavia taught art lessons and grant money dribbled in from various science and educational foundations. He did not return to MIT.

In general, both Devin and Octavia thought that they were happier and less lonely than they would have been in most lives they could have chosen.

She wore grayed frocks and, on the occasions that the evenings got chilly, baggy oversized sweaters. She wore a bright orange hat, floppy brimmed and rounded over her head, that she had bought at a hunting and fishing store back visiting Devin's family in Ohio.

She had said, "It makes me feel safe," and pulled the brim down around her ears. "It doesn't matter anyway. What I wear. I'm an *artist*."

He had liked the way the hat highlighted the paleness of her skin, skin that seemed unaffected by the Honduran sun, and her large grey eyes. He knew that when they returned home to La Ceiba what she wore wouldn't matter because they were privileged foreigners still and lived unquestioned and excused, except to each other.

After twenty years in one of the best butterfly collecting countries in the world, more display walls had grown up across the floor of La Casa de las Mariposas and they hung heavy with shallow, glassed mounting boxes. Devin had his Sphingidae with the longest proboscis in the world. His *Thysania agrippina* had the largest recorded wingspan in the Americas. The butterflies of the Philippines, Madagascar, Papua New Guinea and Portugal, trades from his "World Wide Bug Buddies" as Octavia called them, populated one section of the house. Like a button collection, tiny, winged beetles covered another.

Glancing up from his desk in La Casa, Devin was often surprised to see all the butterflies paused in their exodus to the sky. The sense of flight arrested gave him the same nauseous feeling as being in the passenger seat when the breaks are suddenly slammed on.

If Octavia was well rested she could stand coming into La Casa. She stood very close to the display cases, watching a single insect at a time. When Devin went to the jungle to hunt butterflies she came along and set up her easel on the path. Often too many moths fluttered around her head, and they had to go home before he was ready.

"You don't have to come with," he began to say.

"I like to see you out here where you are so happy," she said.

Once he said, "Paint a picture of me out there, then, and hang it on the wall. That's where all the happy things end up."

Later he said, "I'm sorry. I didn't mean it."

"Yes, you did," she said, her voice unaccusing, flat with fact.

"I don't mean it all the time," he said.

Tourists and groups of school children came to La Casa.

Tourists said, "Oh, I went to that butterfly place in Copan. Amazing. With the larva. Alive. Oh. And they had this one. With the owl-eye wings. Alive."

"Yes," he said.

"But I guess you just like to collect them like this. Dead. To keep them."

"Yes," he said and imagined smashing the glass panes on all the mounted boxes, the butterflies and beetles flapping their wings, rising up, the strength of the hundreds of them lifting the roof from the building.

Octavia, when she could tolerate La Casa, sometimes took photos of individual specimen and made Butterfly Alphabet and Butterfly Number posters from patterns in wing markings. She made postcards. Once when she was drunk and trying to be kind she said La Casa was filled with the solidified notes of children's laughter. Then she shuddered and went for another beer.

"Honey, what are those?" Octavia came into La Casa unexpectedly and stood with her back to the walls of butterflies, looking at Devin.

In a plastic Tupperware dish on his desk were two large beetles. One sucked on the wide, flat side of a mango pit, covering the entire disk with its body. The other one ran again and again against the rounded side of the dish. Pinchers, curved and as thick as his thumb, protruded from their black heads.

"Scarabaeidae Lucanidae," he said.

"Honey."

"They don't fly."

"Are you going to kill them?"

"I already have them in the cases."

"Devin."

"I think they are going to mate. Then they will die."

She rubbed her eyebrow.

"I thought it would be good for the Casa. Everyone comes in and…" He gestured at the walls. "For the kids. To see something alive."

"We are having a party tonight."

"Why?"

"For," she glanced around and dropped her voice low, "the photo."

"Octavia."

Several weeks before she had taken a series of photos of a cloud bank. In one image, the shape of the clouds appeared to spell *Dios*, God in Spanish, and streams of light poured out from behind the cloud letters at the viewer. Octavia was convinced that the image would sell. Pulling a chunk of her small savings, she made poster-sized prints and started rumors with the local churches about a divine image, a message. She had done it without telling Devin and when she finally showed him the prints she had said, "It's going to be big."

"It's something new," she said.

Devin sighed.

"The party's starting with a prayer service. Come at least to that, will you?"

"A prayer service?"

"I'm not arguing about it again. The butterfly number charts are a huge success, aren't they?

"I'm not sure about 'huge,' honey."

"Clouds is a better market. The padre from Luz del Cristo's coming."

"It's just so much money into this picture."

"Don't say picture so loud. I don't want anyone to steal it. And this is on my list, Devin."

"What?"

"My list. Fame."

"Octavia. Ok. But a prayer service?"

"For sales. And perhaps, maybe, God sent this picture and we should be grateful to him. It. To her. Dios."

"We don't.…We've never done that. God."

She glanced at the beetles still eating the mango and bumping the side of the dish.

"We don't do alive either," she said and went into their house.

For the next two weeks, until they died, he watched the beetles for hours each day. Then he nursed their larva towards gestation and brought home two praying mantises.

Octavia visited all the evangelical churches. She began to hum hymns and, occasionally, while brushing her teeth, clapped her hand against her thigh as if she were holding a tambourine. She kept the *Dios* posters in their safe.

In their final stages of development the *Tropidacris violaceus*, stickish, red and purple grasshoppers the length of a child's forearm, developed wings. Devin was hiding them under his desk in La Casa. Sometimes when tourists came he'd say, "Wanna see something?" and pull the insects out, glancing at the door. "They call them saltamontes. Mountain leapers."

One day, while he and a British couple hovered over the plastic cage, Octavia came in carrying a *Dios* poster.

"Hi," she said, "I thought that you had some people back here. They might be interested in looking at this print."

Devin and the couple turned to look at Octavia. Someone's arm knocked the lid off the cage and the saltamontes rose up, leaping impossible distances, wings fluttering to keep them aloft.

After the screaming stopped and the couple left and the print was rerolled, Devin said, "Maybe one of us shouldn't be here."

"I thought that our lives, so small, doing what we want, would make everything stable. There is so little to imbalance. But look how fragile," she said.

"I'm not doing what I want."

"Yes. There are limits to compromise."

"Our lives are too small," he said, though he didn't really know what he meant by it.

"I want you to know that I don't owe you anything," she said.

"No," he looked away from her. "Why would you say something like that?"

"Okay," she said. "I'll be the one to go."

The first postcard came one month later. It was of a church in Matagalpa, Nicaragua. She wrote to him:

I have painted this church. In watercolor.
It is successful but less dreamlike
than I had intended.

Over the past twenty years, every time they traveled, to other cities, to tiny tourist sights and art galleries, Octavia bought postcards with the intention of sending them to her family and friends. Sometimes, when she was anxious she would say out of the blue, "Shoot. I need to send those postcards," but she never did. She packed all of them when she left and went to stay with her sister, Rachel, in the States. Devin had no recollection of visiting the Nicaraguan church, though he knew he must have and the postcard gave him the odd sensation of listening to someone tell a very intimate story about himself that he could not remember.

The next card he received said:

The ocean here is always grey. How
could I forget that?

The image was of parrots on a Mayan ruin, the name *Copán* scrawled across the bottom in white letters gilt blue. He pictured her at the sea, hair wind-tangled beneath the orange hat. He wondered if she had sent the parrots, six flighted animals, as a gift.

The next five postcards, all from different Mayan ruins, no birds, he did not read for two weeks. Then he did, sitting in La Casa, the bodies of the spent saltamontes lying dead in front of him.

I've registered my address at Rachel's.
AARP found me and won't stop sending
magazines. People who are not having
sex at 60 are very unlikely to knock
boots ever again, they say.

He imagined her shock every time an AARP magazine arrived in the mailbox, the covers, the happily mature faces grinning at her with earnest health and words like, Making the Most of Your 401K or Unraveling Medicare Part D or Vacationing with Mobility Scooters. Whenever they had gone back to the States the magazines at the grocery store, filled with foreign concerns, made him unsure of himself. He knew she could not feel anything like those glossy people on the cover.

> *I have taken up with a little sister.*
> *What an upsettingly hopeful thing to*
> *call a program. Big Sister. Big Brother.*
> *Her name is Precious.*

Then:

> *Rachel's dog lost a leg, did you*
> *Know? Yet it balances so well.*

Then:

> *Precious has lived here always,*
> *seven years. Today she saw*
> *the ocean for the first time.*
> *She wants to surf.*

He paused to calculate, collectively, the number of miles the postcards had traveled since Octavia bought them. It was hard to do the calculations. The postcard images made him muddled with remembered feelings. He worked to focus on what was happening now.

> *I have taken a lover.*

Then:

> *Please know that it is*
> *out of fear, not a lack*
> *of love for you.*

Devin continued his life as normal, except he told Fatima, their empleada, that he would pay her but she did not need to come and he scheduled no butterfly catching trips. If people asked, he said that Octavia had gone to visit family. When they arrived he never pretended he would not read the postcards.

Two days later on the house of Rubén Darío:

> *Rachel has a head cold. She*
> *is not friendly. I asked him*
> *to come to me tonight dressed*
> *as a butterfly. How strange*
> *the things that we want.*

To the next card, a picture of the ocean somewhere in Belize, Octavia had taped a piece of her to-do life list, graph paper covered in a row of dark lines striking through words, rendering the words unknowable. In tiny letters next to the stamp she had written:

> *These are some*
> *of the things*
> *I've done.*

Devin remembered drinking something delicious made out of mangoes in Belize and he cried a little. After that he tried not to look at the pictures on the postcards.

> *I'm staying at Ruth's. She's*
> *out of town for a while.*
> *There is a lion in the*
> *house. It lives on the*
> *sofa.*

A week later:

> *The thing is, the lion is*

> *so much more comfortable*
> *there than me. So I've let it*
> *stay. Buying a quarter of a*
> *cow is not economical. I'm*
> *going to look into swine.*

He called Rachel. Yes, she said, a lion. That's what Octavia says. The lion had walked up the stairwell, perhaps lost from some person's private collection, you know how this town is, and flopped down on the couch. Octavia wouldn't hear of calling animal control but had moved back in with Rachel and went every day to feed the thing.

"You know how Octavia is," said Rachel. "You were right not to call her. By the way, she's sold a bunch of those prints. With the clouds."

> *I killed the lion today.*
> *With the machete that*
> *Rodolfo gave me at the*
> *despedida. It was time.*

Then:

> *Not really, but in a way I did.*
> *Kill him. It was time.*

The next day:

> *I painted him. The lion. Not*
> *the lover. With butterfly wings,*
> *flying over the canopy at montaña*
> *de Yoro. Te extraño. But not*
> *in English.*

Devin went out. He sat in the Parque Central until dark came. He re-read all of the cards. They had traveled a collective 89,753 miles, from kiosks and historical sites, to La Ceiba, to the States, to La Ceiba, to get to him. A Garifuna woman sold him bread and a man named Frankie, homeless the twenty-five years Devin had been in La Ceiba, came up and asked in English as he always did, "Where you from?"

"Here, Frankie,"

"No man. New York. The Big Apple." He spread his arm wide. "King of the Hill. A-number-one. The Big Apple."

"Yeah, Frankie."

"Ain't from here."

Devon gave Frankie the bread and walked to the central market. A carnival was set up with shooting games and lotería and stalls of fried food. A Ferris wheel turned in a rickety circle. On the far edge stood a ride that had eight cars, each a different shape. Octopussing arms attached each car to the main mechanism. Dark had fallen and a row of lights filled up the arms like suckers. He paid for a ticket, pretending to not understand Spanish when the ride owner explained it was for children. Devon walked around the machine and found a car in the shape of an airplane, a smiling face painted on its nose. His legs hardly fit and he sat with his knees tucked up against his chest. When it started the ride made a loud clunk and then whirred as it worked to get off the ground. Devin and seven children floated up into the sky, their hair whipping back, cresting again and again as the cars rode through the air as if hopping waves. He held the postcards up into the night sky and, when he let them go, the colors in the photographs glimmered, flitting, reflecting the lights of the flying machine.

FUN LAND

I think Ione never hopes that something truly terrible will happen. I think she never fantasizes about a terrorist cell leaking cyanide into the cotton candy machines or an electric malfunction that forces open the safety restraints on all the rides as the cars hit corkscrew turns, forces the teacups into an uncontrollable frenzy until they rocket from their chassis and project passengers towards large, blunt objects. Ione is a Buddha, content with the stumbles, with the heat exhaustion, with the nicks and scrapes and over stimulation and stomach flus, able to treat each child wandering and unmoored from a legal guardian with the serious care of a possible child abandonment case, with thoughtful discretion and, then, smile with true warmth at each reunification, even the reunifications where parents promise to wallop their kids for wandering off, even the ones where parents wallop their kids for wandering off, right there in front of us, careful to use the palms of their hand so we have no justification for contacting Child Protective Services. Her care and love and professionalism is an even, perfect blanket, big enough to cover everyone who comes, carried on blasts of hot summer air, into our cooled aid station trailer.

I am not like Ione. I fantasize about a world in which all the parents really do disappear and Ione and I pull two folding chairs and a cooler of juice boxes out of the aid station, sit down and watch the unruled children form factions and cults, commit sacrifices upon the Hay Maker. Sometimes, when confronted with a lost kid, I subvocalize, "Maybe Mommy did leave you, Jimmy. Ever really consider that?"

I don't think I am cruel. Just bored.

The park opens at 11 and at 11:30 this morning we have two wailing children, the parents of the wailing children and a woozy adult. I have diagnosed the woozy adult with a hangover and the children with missed naps. The parents of the children worry about some effect that the rides might have had on the internal organs of their children.

"Has your child had an unusual schedule today? Have you deviated from the norm?" I ask the parents of one child.

"Right after we got off the ride, the boat, the swinging boat, he started crying."

"When did you get on the swinging boat?"

"I don't know."

"It's 11:30am now."

"Oh maybe. 11:15. There was a line. We thought the park opened at 10 so we have been waiting."

"What is Susie normally doing, on a normal day, at 11am?"

"What? The ride."

"If you were not here. At home."

"What? At the nanny. She takes a nap, I guess. At day care. She is so upset. Look at her. Perhaps she is in pain. Susie. Where does it hurt?"

Both kids are sobbing harder now and I can see the other set of parents leaning forward, about to get in on the conversation.

"I am no parent," I say, "but I am a nurse and I'm going to offer a radical idea. Is it possible that this missed nap is the problem? Had you considered?"

Behind me, as I knew I would, I hear Ione's chair roll away from her desk where she's patiently completing paperwork. She stands beside me and glances at the sign in sheet to get the parents' name.

"Mrs. Richards. It's so common here at Fun Land that patrons forget their regular life, the excitement, the stimulation. The park is great, well, fun, but it can really overwhelm kids. And I'm guessing you are traveling? Yes? It is so easy, when we travel, to get away from our regular schedule. Of course we want to take Susie's experience very seriously. You are her parent. You know her best. So why don't you stay here for ten minutes. In the cool air where we can monitor her and see how it goes?" And Ione slides a Fun Land coloring book and a juice box and crackers across the desk. Her action has the feel of authority and great service and someone offering a bribe they know will be taken.

"Thank you so much," says Mrs. Richards to Ione.

Ione and I do not acknowledge her intervention and I turn to the hangover case, ignoring the other child.

"So you drank heavily last night and then decided to start the day with the Dervish of Fun?"

"Yes. But I've been drunk before, you know. But this is different."

"Really?" I say.

He nods miserably.

"Is that because you don't normally start your day with the Dervish of Fun?" I say, listening for Ione to shift towards us. She does not usually intervene on adult cases, but since she is already standing she might.

The aid station walkie-talkie crackles, "BA15 at Big Wave. BA15 at Big Wave."

There has been an injury and the B indicates that it's more than hysterics but not time to call the paramedics. The A indicated that the injured party is proving generally friendly and not throwing punches. 15 is a guess at the age of the injured party.

"Ten bucks it's a teenage boy who jumped off the platform to impress his friends instead of using the steps. Sprained ankle," I mutter to Ione.

"Would you mind taking it, Clarice. I can take care of all this," she indicates the hangover and the sniffling children.

This is Ione's secret. She has all the patience in the world but she hates to go out there, out into the screaming and the 16-year-olds cutting the line and the sticky concrete and all the dazzling, dazzling sun. I think, basically, for her, it's like walking through *Apocalypse Now* and she's never hopped up on anything to help her get through the humans and machines she cannot control.

"Sure," I say.

It's a sprained ankle.

"Trying to show off to your friends," I say to the kid.

"Yeah," says the kid.

"Yeah," I say.

He has terrible acne and will be very handsome in about ten years but does not know it. When we get him back to the aid station trailer a girl, already pretty, from his group of friends, almost stays with him but then does not, promising to check back in in a while. He lays on a cot, ankle elevated, till he can't stand not being with his friends and hobbles off, ignoring our advice.

If a D-call (call the paramedics) comes through, Ione reaches for the telephone.

"Would you mind going out to them? Would you mind? I'm closer to the phone here, to call dispatch."

Her confident and apologetic actions say, "Would you mind?" with the knowledge that I will go out the door and she will stay and call dispatch and the knowledge that she needs it to be that way. We have never talked about how she tenses a little when the door opens, revealing the dirty concrete walkway and the glare of sunlight, how she relaxes again when the door latch clunks shut.

"Sure," I always say, and grab the emergency kit.

Later she says, "Don't forget the paperwork."

She worries about me making a mistake on the paperwork, about the litigious nature of the world and keeping her job. I do not believe she worries about my medical knowledge or my ability to stay cool and calm in a crisis. I stay cool and calm in a crisis. I hate the paperwork.

The park has been sued, on several occasions, for injury, pain and suffering. Fun Land has settled out of court each time. Never have I or, so far as I know, Ione, been asked to explain our records.

This is my tenth summer as a nurse at Fun Land. Fun Land has been open for one-hundred-and-five years.

There used to be a ride here when it first opened, where people waited in long lines winding up high staircases. At the top they straddled metal horses fixed to tracks and the horses flew down to the earth, people's hair streaming back, top hats lifting off heads. On the ground once more, the riders walked a path paved with metal grates. Air blew through the grates. Women's skirts billowed, ankles and knees and thighs exposed even as the women shied away. Also, along this path little people with cattle prods waylaid the riders, chased them, shocked them with the electrodes. Bleachers rose alongside the path and anyone who wanted could sit and watch for women's ankles to emerge from wafting cloth and for cattle prods to make contact. I know all of this because of a photograph, large, black-and-white, imposingly framed, that hangs in the main office. All these things are happening and, on the card underneath it says, *The Pony Ride, Fun Land, 1914*. The photo hangs next to images of Sam, the Fun Land Clam, our mascot, and the park's oldest ride, The Turbulent Train, and a smiling color portrait of our current CEO. Nothing on the card or anywhere else mentions that The Pony Ride is really weird. Nothing mentions that it plays on our desires for voyeurism, pain, vulnerability and profanity. It does not mention how, in comparison, our current rides are a little one-dimensional. All that pain and vulnerability, the fear and submission, those things now happen to riders in relative isolation, no witness, or it happens in a group, a car full, all the people submitting and in fear together but we don't offer much opportunity for voyeurism, unless you buy the photo of yourself that the automated camera took as you started into the big loop. It might be more popular if we offered photos of other people, the stricken faces of strangers, for sale.

I'm not sure what they did for first aid back then. Probably not much.

When it's Ione's lunch, her husband, Tommy, will come by if he can. He's the Lead Engineering Manager and I'm pretty sure that's why Ione's still here. A hold over in the budget. An RN is pricey compared with a health aid worker. Two RN's are very pricy and I am still here because Ione needs me to go outside into the park when the emergencies happen. I come because the money is easy. A shift at Fun Land is nothing compared to the peds ward at the hospital. I keep showing up every summer and they keep paying me. In the main area of the aid station trailer, when Tommy comes by, Ione's blanket of calm and consideration covers her husband with the same perfect evenness as everyone else. If one of the two exam/relaxation rooms are open, though, they will excuse themselves to go "take their lunch" in the room. Ione says things like "take our lunch." I'm sure while they are in there they are messing around, they are silently pumping away on the vinyl cots. If I had to lay money on it, I'd offer odds that Ione gives some pretty impressive head, even after 20 years with Tommy. I know that if I opened the door while they were "taking their lunch" and asked her to convince parents that the consumption of three deep-fried snickers might be the cause of a child's stomach pain, Ione could turn and inspire grateful confidence from the parents at the same time as monitoring and encouraging Tommy's movement towards climax. I can't actually hold the two thoughts in my head at once, though, both of these Iones. When I think of Ione gently pinching her husband's thighs, Ione offering free packets of sunscreen flees from my mind.

Occasionally we get something complicated. A compound fracture. People unconscious due to head trauma or heat exhaustion. Twice fights got bad enough that one person stabbed another person with a knife they had smuggled in. No one has died. Not in my ten years.

At three in the afternoon we hear an explosion.

"That was an explosion," I say.

D-calls start coming in through the walkie-talkie and the voices are panicked. They don't say, "DB35." They say, "Call 911." They say, "Call for help." They shout and the sound is staticky and distorted. The screaming coming straight through the trailer walls indicates the same directive.

Had I thought about it I would not have thought that there was so much to burn. Fun Land seemed like a barren land populated with only spidery metal structures. After the explosion, thought, with the drought and extreme heat and the wind, all these factors larger than us, the place burned. Awnings and seats. Teddy bear prizes. All lit up like Christmas.

Twenty-four people died. 153 injured. I am out in it running triage.

The truth is that, when I opened the door of the aid station trailer and looked out at all the people running, the panic, the fire, the screams coming from the apex of the carousel, it all looked familiar.

It took until my second or third summer at Fun Land to start fantasizing disaster. My second or third summer of stomach flus and over-stimulated children. I never have such visions at the pediatric ward, but in the trailer at Fun Land I find myself imagining gunshot wounds and mass chaos. It does not matter why, boredom, regret, when I walk through the parking lot towards the employee entrance gap in the fence, I wish for high-speed chases to ensue, to force me to duck under cars, crawl towards Ronny, Maintenance Engineer, who is frozen with fear, and pull him down to protect him from the spray of bullets. What matters is that I wished this kind of disaster. I thought it. I tasted and smelled it. Sometimes I fell asleep at night to visions of hyper-contagious plagues circling the park, roller coaster after roller coaster falling silent as operators succumbed.

I have made it real. Real. Real. You can only hope things so much, so many time, so many years, before you get them.

Once, when I was a kid, I made a face and it stayed that way. My cheek muscles knotted up and I had to go to the doctor to get a shot to relax them again. There was a sort of sweetness to the pain, to the fulfillment of the threat that if I made that face it would stay that way.

"We need you in here, Ione," I told her after I opened the door and saw the fire and the people running and the sun still bright before all the smoke clouded over it. I am grateful that I had the presence of mind to tell her to stay in. Ione, always at work before the gates open, staying till the crowds thin. Ione. I could not spare the dead, the burned. I could spare Ione from the screaming panic outside.

Twenty-four dead, 153 injured. The park, after 105 years, is shut indefinitely.

I did rise to the occasion. I was calm and collected. I did help set evacuation procedures in place, tend the wounded, assign roles, communicate clearly with outside emergency medical professionals. I did triage. I did pull a few patrons from burning places. I kept several people from shock.

It was thrilling. When children are lost from their parents in the middle of a raging field of fire one must respond with worry and care. Smoke inhalation causes unconsciousness and vomiting.

When they present me with an award, when I come up to take the award, a plaque glued to a shining chunk of something that may be wood, a microphone looms before me. Someone, a firefighter, maybe an elected official, makes a speech and then applause and then a microphone looms before me and on beyond the microphone is a room full of people circled around white table-clothed tables cluttered with used hors d'oeuvres plates and bottles of beer. I grasp the award. I lean into the microphone.

"Sorry," I say. "Sorry."

I think people applaud when I leave the stage.

I go to the media with the truth. *Dear Diane Wilchers of Local 10 News at 9, I am writing because I feel it is important that the cause of the terrible events at Fun Land be explained. I am one of two registered nurses that were on duty when the explosion occurred. For years now a low hum, a constant hum of desired destruction has been pervasive in my daily life throughout every summer I have worked. . . .* When the media does not respond I go to social media. On Facebook I post "I caused the death of dozens and the end of Fun Land." I see a few likes and get a few comments that start with, "Oh, hon . . ." I don't read the rest of the comment. I get the list of the twenty-four people dead and 153 injured and send notes of sorrow and condolence. The first drafts explain my culpability and how I caused their loss, how

I imagined and imagined until it became before my eyes. "Too soon," I think. "Too soon for these people." I simply tell them that they can blame me for any failing, fault or lack I demonstrated.

"Please," I write, "blame me."

I cannot look at flowers. It is July and lilies and larkspur still bloom in some yards. When I look at the plants I imagine them withered, withering, the delicate red and purple beauty time lapsed to crumpled and rotting. I know these visions I have will end the blooms too soon. I will think the flowers dead. At intersections I see cars crash against each other and how many times will I imagine this until I make it so? When I think of my mother, my healthy, active mother, pinochle on Wednesdays, woodworking on Thursdays, I think of her rasping on oxygen tubes and an IV inserted into her pale skin and so I cannot call her.

What I can do is go back to Fun Land. I can sit outside the aid station trailer because it did not burn, it remained untouched, sit out and watch the crews that come to secure the area, raze structures that could fall, check gas line. They seal things and bring everything closer to the earth.

I watch the demolition that I created continue. I pull up bits of grass and weed that survived so that everything will be barren. The Turbulent Train burned, its wooden tracks a ring of fire. Sam, The Fun Land Clam made it, though, and from where I sit can see him, goggle-eyed, up on top of the unharmed entrance booths.

Ione calls. She calls and calls. Maybe she only calls once. Twice. Three-hundred times. Ione. When she calls I feel her endless calm, her blanket across the aid station. I become nauseous.

"Please call," she says on the voice mails. And maybe her husband Tommy talks also, "Please call."

She does not come to the awards ceremony. I cannot see anyone's face clearly. I do not know who is there at the tables with the dirty dishes but I can see that she is not there. Clearly she is not there.

At Fun Land I cannot look at the work crews, only at the weeds and the slowly devolving rides. Once I look at the workers and imagine an earthquake shaking, shaking the unstable structures, the men in their useless orange vests stumbling to the ground and the steal arms of the Octo-Fun crashing, pinning them down.

We don't have earthquakes here. We live on one of those profound faults that rarely shifts but, they say, has the potential to wipe several states from the map, to tear the continent in pieces.

I make sure I look official sitting outside the trailer. It is a skill I have developed, looking purposeful and busy while doing nothing. In a hospital it is sometimes the only way you can get a break. If you really need a breather, need to not go to another patient room, answer another phone, you get this thing where you hold a chart and keep your shoulders tense and a look of focus on your face, the brow and edges of lips slightly contracted, while you think about the life cycle of bees or the laundry or different whitenesses of paper.

When a drone is no longer useful to the hive, when he is simply eating and without potential to mate the queen, he is dragged, by the worker bees, from the hive to perish. That is a thing I learned once and a thing I think while I sit outside the trailer and look very busy. I am not obvious about pulling up the weeds. No one questions me.

Besides the workers demolishing unsafe structures other men come out. They hold clipboards and various scientific tools and look very busy. They are not considering the future, they are not concerned with rebuilding or unbuilding. They are like historians. They wander the site, reconstruct past events and try to understand the original cause, the original system failure or mistake. Maybe they interview other witnesses but they never interview me. I sit by the emergency health trailer and sweat cold sweat while they pick through the tangle. I am desperate for them to come so I can tell them the truth. I am full of terror that they would come and I would tell them the truth. I am what they are looking for, a cause. How many times, for how many years, did I see, did I yearn, how many times, the explosion, the soot on cheekbones. I yearned for something to happen and now it has happened.

A construction worker cuts his arm badly on some jagged metal. He comes to see me, his arm held out. He is calm, perhaps because of some previous experience with having a seemingly uninterested object slice his skin and expose his muscle or perhaps because he is calm. CA35 I think to myself.

I should not treat him. I am not quite a Samaritan, I think, sitting in front of the trailer with my ID hooked to my scrubs. I am not contracted, hired, supported with liability insurance but I am wearing my ID clipped to my chest.

He must go to the ER. It will be better if I can bandage him some first. I turn and open the door to the trailer which, I find, is unlocked. I have not been in since the day of the accident when I went to get Ione and, after all the paramedics had left and the evacuation was mostly finished, when everything was calmer, held her arm hard and looked in her eyes and said, "Come on," and walked her out to the parking lot, concentrating on the firmness of my body, the steadiness of my walk so that she did not have to be firm and steady.

I would have been embarrassed if the door had not opened. I did not expect it to open. I had assumed that someone had locked it after the explosion. How, though, would I have explained my presence, day after day, to this bleeding man if the door was locked? Inside it smells still of smoke and of garbage that had not been brought out.

"Here." I sit him on an exam/rest bed and pull out gloves and sterile pads.

"Silly of me," he says.

"Maybe," I say. "We are all silly sometimes."

He goes to say something else.

"Hush," I say. "Save your strength."

"Who will drive you to the ER?" I say.

"I'll be fine. I'll drive myself."

"No. You should not. I'll take you."

"Elevate your arm," I say when I have him in the passenger's seat.

"Of course," he says.

I make sure that another demolition worker has his keys and will get his car home.

I solve all the problems. There would not be this gash in this arm, this abandonment of a car, without the initial problem, the initial explosion. All my dreams.

One-hundred percent of the dead were under eighteen because this is an amusement park. Two of them had been in the aid trailer earlier in the day.

What happens when you cause such destruction as this? Jail? Seizure of assets? What empty actions those feel. What does locking me away, making me homeless, have to do with such horror? How could that bring solace to the families? How could that bring solace to me?

Every week when it arrives I pull the rubber band off the small, local newspaper, curled like a snail shell, and skim through for news on the injured, on the property damage.

Three months out I open the paper to find that the report has been published and the assessors have named the park liable for damages due to negligence and the Lead Engineer will be charged with willful misconduct.

The thing about love songs is that when you are not in love they sound like songs of sorrow. So slow. So nostalgic.

The Lead Engineer is Tommy. Tommy and Ione in the exam/relaxation room taking their lunch.

Fun Land. There is a song:

Fun Land. Fun Land./ Welcome to our one land /where the children play/ day 'o after day.

There are other verses.

Every year a weekend-long marching band competition happens at Fun Land and each of the several dozen bands has to play the "Fun Land Song" as part of their repertoire.

Nostalgia is a strange thing. This year there will be no marching band competition and I will miss hearing the song. The terrible, terrible song.

After going into the aid trailer to find bandages for the injured demolisher and taking him to the ER, I go in to the aid trailer every day to sit behind the check-in desk, a high wall that had arrived one morning, years ago, after a drunk and terribly sunburned man launched himself at Ione when she informed him that we did not have any way to make or fill prescriptions. She told him that we could, in fact, only advise basic over the counter remedies but not offer them and he came right at her. I sit everyday behind the check-in counter and I am not sure if I am waiting.

When the demolishers finish and leave, if you walk the chain link fence around Fun Land, like most chain link fences, you can find a place where people have hacked at the wire, clean cuts in this case. You can push against the fence and emerge behind the remains of the Flying Shoe.

In August and even days in September the air inside the aluminum and vinyl trailer presses close and hot. I sit behind the desk until my head begins to spin and then, leaning on the walls, stumble outside onto the relative cool of the dirt and char and concrete.

By October it is very, very cold inside. There are no cloth surfaces. Only plastics and metal, built for sterility and summer. Each day I let myself into the trailer expecting to find people squatting, to be hit over the head, solicited, asked to attend an injury. No one is inside except me.

It is almost Halloween and days and days ago I read about Tommy. I sit at the desk until I shiver and then I pick up the telephone receiver.

I had not done that yet and when I hear a dial tone come through everything goes a little sideways because of how little I understand about how things work. Since the explosion there has been no electricity in the park. But the phone works. Who pays for it? Who has called?

I dial Ione's number. She answers. I say nothing. I hang up. She will, of course, know the number, see it on her caller ID. Will she think about the safety of this inside place? Will she think of the explosion? Will she scream to her husband, a man wrongfully accused? Will she wait patiently for another call to come?

The thought of her, hands in lap, eyes alert to everything, waiting quietly by the phone makes the skin under my fingernails hurt so I call again.

"I've worried about you," she says.

"I saw the newspaper."

"Yes."

"He is innocent."

"Yes. Well. Thank you. It might be complicated."

"I believe that you should blame me."

"Clarice."

"The press would not publish my confession, but you must know. You know. After all our time together."

"It's very serious for us right now. I'm not really able to talk about it but they are putting together a strong case."

I had read in the paper about how they had found a correlation between diminished revenue and delinquent maintenance.

"Tommy never wanted anything, you never wanted anything, but for people to be safe," I said.

"Yes. Yes. Of course."

"If you'd like I'd like to come by and explain it all."

"Oh."

"Yes. Please."

"We have worried about you, but."

"Yes."

Ione's house is very floral patterned and clean. The colors are mostly cream or intentionally faded. The distance from living room door, across the thick white carpet to the wicker couch feels like a very long way. She does not, on the wall, have a cuckoo clock that ticks loudly but she should. I hear the sound ticking in my head anyway and if she could also it would help fill the space as we sit and look at each other.

"Is Tommy here?" I ask.

"Oh." Ione is a bad liar and she knows it. "Yes."

When Tommy comes in it is all very polite. Hello, hello. Lovely to see you. Tommy and Ione do not look at each other.

"It is not your fault," I say.

Tommy says nothing.

"It is my fault," I say.

All that smoke billowing up. How does a roller coaster catch on fire? Something about electricity burning. When it is hot enough so many things are flammable that one would not expect. The whole world. The whole wide world. Everything has a point where it will come busting apart. Glory or something. A horror of ugly.

I know that I want them to find a cancer in my lungs. Now. In five years. Even if it is in five years I'll know it is from all that smoke, all those particles of roller coaster busting apart that I breathed. It will be less, all those deaths I made, when I have the lung cancer. They will weigh less, balanced against my illness.

"In all the fire and how it smelled I had done that. It's me, Tommy. Ione knows. Ask her."

"Please go," says Ione. "Please go."

Such a thing. Such a direct thing to say to me. To anyone.

All those parents that shouted at us for the past ten years. The men that vomited on our shoes and puckered up their mouths like suckling babies and said, "Nurse me, sweetie." All that and Ione had never said anything so direct.

"Put me on the stand," I say. "I'd like to explain it. My influence."

"Please go," says Ione.

Tommy sits, his big mass perched on the edge of a stiff-cushioned chair, the cushion creased in just along the top edge. He balances, one leg forward, one leg back, a tripod, ready to topple, launch forward. I reach towards his hands.

"No," says Ione.

"I don't think I understand," says Tommy. He looks at me with a little bit of hope in his wide face.

"I wanted it. I saw it. So many times. Something to do, I suppose. But you can only imagine a thing so many times before it becomes."

"What did you do?" says Tommy.

"I made it," I say. "And now I cannot unmake it."

"What did you do?" says Tommy.

"I wanted it. There was something where I wanted it. Something. So now it is. All the time it is. All these years, Tommy. I made you do it."

"Stop," says Ione. She is well trained in leveraging bodyweight and I am up and across the floor, propelled with her to the door. I lock my knees but the momentum is too great and then I am outside.

The demolisher who cut his arm and I sit in the ER. He said he was fine to go in alone, but I go in with him.

"Let me talk with them," I say.

There are words that get you past the desk faster, ways of expressing urgency and language that shows you are of the place, that you know what's necessary.

Medical professionals know each other, a certain confidence, a tone, fluency with the lingo.

"I'll handle this," I say.

At the desk sits the charge nurse.

"There has been an accident," I say. It does not sound correct. It is not the correct, inside language.

"They have been cleaning up from an accident and there has been an accident."

The nurse continues to look at me. Doors are not opening.

"Please," I say.

And then I notice the ER waiting room for the first time. When we entered through the sliding door, woosh, into the AC, the worker and I,

I only noticed the chair he could sit in and the front desk. Points, dots in space that I needed to connect. Now the waiting room comes into full view. Clusters of chairs like the Tennessee Spinner. The wounded and ill leaning on them like riders fighting centrifugal force. A wheelchair and two empty gurneys wait against the wall by the big swinging doors that lead to inside. The gurneys look discarded and useless.

The room seems filled with screams. I cannot tell if the screaming is always there, ambient noise, or specific to this moment. It is so hard to explain the difference between screams of terror and screams of delighted terror. Maybe there is no difference. Maybe the difference is that you know there has been an explosion, burns, fractures, that the cause of the fear is not contained or controlled, then after you know you hear the screams different. Maybe they are actually different. In the ER I cannot tell.

"There has been an explosion and a fire. It was not an accident. There was a cause. But this man was cleaning up and now he needs a doctor right now," I say to the charge nurse.

The man and I sit and wait. Around and around and around us the chairs spin and the faces of our neighbors distort in suffering and delight.

"Had you been to Fun Land, before?" I ask.

"I grew up here," he says. He begins to sing. "*Fun Land. Fun Land./ Welcome to our one land.*"

Because he is in a lot of pain, I don't start to cry. I don't shout at him to shut up.

"I'm fine," he insists.

"It's better to have someone with you. I will stay with you," I tell him.

He says nothing.

"It is better," I tell him. "It is better that I stay."

SEX ED

One afternoon in the 5th grade the boys and the girls were cleaved from each other.

The Boys

We were shuffled from the gym into a classroom and, after a few minutes, Mr. Millins wheeled in the TV cart. A movie. A real treat. He bent and grunted, plugged in the VCR and the TV. He pushed in a tape and then ambled to the back of the room and sat in one of the child-sized seats.

We watched a single, unbroken shot. The camera did not move. We struggled to define the image. Through context clues, the identification of thighs, of a butt, we understood that we looked at a vagina. For most of us this was our first vagina. It was furry and confusing. Just as we identified the object it transformed, stretching, screaming, blood and shit and undefined muck, like snot, like pudding, there on the screen. The vagina shit itself. Some other thing, some other harry flesh emerged from the vagina and retracted, emerge and retracted. The other thing became a head, a head like an old man, a head like an alien covered in snot and blood and hands pulled a baby from the vagina. We thought the movie would end now but it began again, the stretching and screaming and the vagina pushed out a chunk of something misformed, dead.

Mr. Millins paced silently to the TV cart, held down the rewind button and we watched the dead thing and the mucky, skinny baby and the blood and shit and snot go back into the vagina and then Mr. Millins took his finger off the rewind button and we saw it all again. After the dead thing came out of the vagina a second time, Mr. Millins unplugged everything and wheeled the TV cart out. For several minutes we sat quiet, unsupervised. Mr. Millins returned.

"Go to the lunchroom," he said. "Single file."

The Girls

They took the boys away and we were left in the cavernous gym. We, all, had been seated together so, when the boys left, gaps existed between us, girls adrift and stranded cross-legged on the shellacked wood. They were saving energy a lot that year so the lights remained mostly off except one row of florescent tubes on the far edge of the ceiling.

Ms. Jenevieve said, "Girls, we have a special visitor."

A nun came and stood in front of us.

The nun spoke about how she had been a fallen woman. How she had made a baby inside her. How she had birthed the baby and how the baby had been taken from her so that it could have a better life. She told us she had become a nun when she was eighteen. The way she talked, the inflection, we expected her to touch her belly but her hands always stayed stretched a few inches to the sides of her body.

She spoke and, if we leaned the right way, we could make it so that, from our perspective, her head blotted out the basketball hoop behind her.

Ms. Jenevieve said, "Sit still," in the same yelling tone that our mothers used if they were scared we were going to tumble out of a third-story window.

The nun went to the big double doors of the gym and opened one and wheeled a trolley back to where she had been standing. The trolley had a tall something on it covered with a sheet. She pulled the sheet off and revealed a bloody, skinny Jesus. He looked upwards, begging for something, rivulets of blood all down his ears and cheeks and nose. He held his hands out a few inches from the sides of his body, the palms full of blood as if he was going to cup his hands and drink.

The nun told us that this was where she found salvation and where she would remain for eternity. We did not know if she showed us the Jesus as an offering or as a threat. She covered up the Jesus and Ms. Jenevieve applauded so we all applauded and the nun wheeled the Jesus out.

Ms. Jenevieve left for a while and then rolled the TV cart in, plugged in everything, turned off the row of lights and started a video.

In the movie, nuns sang in a choir and then the camera zoomed in on a Jesus and then one nun sat in a small room for a while and then the camera zoomed in on a Jesus and then, on top of Jesus's bloody face the screen said *St. Magdalene for the Fallen*, and then the screen went to static.

"All right, girls. Let's head over to the lunchroom," said Ms. Jenevieve and she turned on the one row of lights and we all filed to the lunchroom where they had Capri Sun juice boxes lined up on a table and we each took one and, as gently as possible, punctured a hole in it with the pointed end of the straw. After a minute the boys came in and we made way for them to get to the juice boxes.

Senior Year

We all asked each other to the prom. We went to the high school gym and wondered what would happen, after midnight, in the back seats of cars. We drank juice from plastic Champaign glasses. If we were not careful the long plastic stems of the glasses disconnected from their round bases and toppled over. The tables and floors and our hands became sweet and sticky.

I HAVE TO OFFER FOR YOU
MONEY POWER LOVE

A woman named Celeste has been trying to contact a man named Greg Smith through Lanna's email address. The messages sent to Lanna's email address come several times a week. What she wants to communicate, the woman named Celeste says, is not a joke. Lanna has looked at the messages and finds that the English in the emails reads as formal and, also, curiously unclear. The emails discuss Money Power Love. It is difficult for Lanna to understand if Celeste intends to offer Greg Smith these things themselves or only information about them.

Lanna does not have much experience with this particular trinity, Money Power Love. She has though, lately, been interested in blind faith. It is grey winter, and she has never been any kind of religious and she would like to experience some blind faith. She believes that opening the emails from Celeste, in the face of cybersecurity concerns, demonstrates something akin to blind faith and she finds the act, with each new email, heady and gripping and wants more. As she thinks is the case with most humans, she has a general interest in Money Power Love and she believes Celeste about not being a joke. Joke is not the right word. Celeste is not quite funny and, when Lanna thinks about it, she does feel that if anyone, without causing much harm, has the ability to get more Money Power Love, or more knowledge of Money/Power/Love, they should. So, in an act of blind faith, Lanna decides to work to get Greg Smith and Celeste together.

Lanna has some money in her life. Getting-by-without-too-much-worry-for-now money. It comes in every two weeks from her job that she goes to every Monday-Friday.

Lanna has some love in her life. There are friends and scattered family. She has love with a man she met two months before, while on a vacation, and who lives very far away, far enough that they have to count the difference in their hours, do basic addition and subtraction, each time they plan to see each other. They see each other on their phones on WhatsApp's video feature and he is concerned and thoughtful and has learned about her friends and scattered family. They have jokes together. His English grammar is improving. She is ashamed at how difficult it is for her to retain even a few words of his language and at his patience each time he repeats words for her, saying each syllable slowly and clearly. When they are not talking he sends her pictures of his day, and she understands that they are gifts. She remembers that, in person, he had a way of flopping confident and unaware through the world. He cut in front of people. He spoke over people.

Greg Smith is a common name. This makes for problems. Not problems, Lanna tells herself. Special circumstances. Challenges. Special circumstance challenges in trying to get Celeste and the correct Greg Smith together.

Lanna writes an email. She will send it to lots of Greg Smiths. She figures, as she has no other clues to go on, that working with sheer mass is the best way to find *the* Greg Smith. Lanna wants it to matter, wants Celeste to be reaching out into the world for a very specific Greg Smith, *the* Greg Smith, for whom she possesses very specific somethings about Money Power Love. She wants to believe that Celeste will help Greg Smith, not just attempt to take from him.

Lanna worries the email she has written won't really grab the reader, will not indicate the important point that this is not spam, this is personal, and she especially worries about the subject line.

Subject: Maybe there is something

Dear Greg,

There could be something in this. I have come to believe that there could be something in this and I have not yet seen yet that anything for sure points to this being not true.

What is this? You wonder maybe. What this is is a person named Celeste has the ability to get you something about money and power and love and don't worry because Celeste did not ask me to email you.

Greg Smith respond. I can connect you with Celeste. It seems like a long shot, yes, maybe, but what do you have going on in your life, Greg Smith, that you can turn your nose up and away from getting closer to money and power and love? Do you really need no more of these?

Best,
Lanna

P.S. It could be money or power or love. Or money and power and love and I'm not sure if you will have to choose.

Lanna could just forward Celeste's email, but she wants to be involved. She wants, through her blind faith, to get closer to Money Power Love. She wants to see the transfer. She feels how insisting on being a part of it is a sticky and satisfying selfish thing.

She copy-and-pastes the email to ten Greg Smiths she finds through a google search of "Greg Smith". She does it at home at the table in her studio apartment while the radiator clanks away. She feels tender towards each Greg Smith. The next day she checks her email, breathless, sneaking at work, and after the walk back from the bus, bursting into her apartment where it is warm enough to take her phone out again.

Three emails bounce back, MAILER-DAEMON. On the second day she finds ten more Greg Smiths and cuts and pastes and cuts and pastes and she decides that any Greg Smiths that email back will be the ones. Her's and Celeste's. She will not pick and choose and judge and set criteria and compare and find wanting. Lanna finds it difficult to be resolute in this decision of inclusivity that may be a decision based on boredom and fear and allows herself hope that it does matter, that Celeste seeks a unique Greg Smith.

Her romance that exists on the phone screen exists in a tight frame, mostly only the face of the far away man, held in her hand, without much context. Always her own face, even tinier, is embedded in one corner of the screen. She does not understand that feature, why she should always see herself, as if she were in junior high again, constantly self-aware, untrusting of the person she is talking to, and she cannot turn it off. There can be no eye contact, each of them looking down at their screen, at the image of the other's face and away from the actual cameras at the tops of their phones. Once or twice he asks to let their eyes meet across the ocean. She spends a few moments of silence, staring at the camera in the top of her phone while he, she presumes, stares at his, and then he says, "Thank you," with deep, calm gratitude and she does not tell him how lonely she felt, looking away from his downturned eyes and into the black hole of the lens.

Lanna runs a constant calibration of the effect her face has on his face, tracking the small responses of his eyes and lips to the small movements of hers, taking measurements of his love. She cannot help but monitor the tiny box of her face and light herself for optimal beauty and control her expressions, repressing incredulous eyebrow arches, working to keep her chin up and neck long. At any moment the connection could slow, and she might be frozen on his screen, mouth gaping, cheeks stretched hideous, a part of the sum of a facial expression that one does not notice when a face is in motion. She trains herself away from any vestiges of early childhood, when she did not know what was expected of her face. She knows that this is vanity. She knows that it is petty and silly, and she still makes sure to hold the phone at the best angle, up and to the right, minute after minute. These actions have something, she knows, to do with power. She is in love with how in love he is with her face, in their tight little world. She knows that people fall in love with flaws, rough bits. She cannot help, anyway, wanting to see herself lovely and she cannot help but want to believe that he adores her loveliness. She curates, she maintains the image of herself, sat just above his shoulder or on his chest, to increase his love for her and her love for herself. Whenever the connection drops and her image freezes, pulled, swayed, he takes a screenshot and, delighted, texts it to her. He is not malicious when he does this, but loving, joying in the possibilities of her face. Looking at these pictures Lanna feels something cavernous like despair deep inside, an ache that he would love her more for accidental grotesqueries than her practiced, considered grace.

After three weeks she has sent emails to two hundred Greg Smiths. She hears nothing and, also, the emails from Celeste to Greg Smith stop arriving. Lanna continues to refresh her email often and remains steadfast in feeling that Celeste is still out there, waiting for her Greg Smith.

The man in her phone says, "I want to come to visit you. I try to make it work." She keeps her face very still and says nothing. He begins to tell her of this desire often, with updates on the things hindering the trip—work, money, caring for a sick family member—and what he is doing to solve the problems. He is very earnest and Lanna says nothing.

She considers Facebook and LinkedIn as platforms for connecting with Greg Smith. However, something feels impure about these modes. Celeste used email. So Lanna uses email. One evening, a Tuesday, when it is too late to call the man in the phone and she believes she has emailed four hundred and fifty Greg Smiths and has for sure drunk 2.5 glasses of slightly vinegared wine, so as to not have to dump the bottle, Lanna almost emails Celeste directly. She catches herself, cursor hovered over "reply." In breathless panic and relief she closes and hugs her laptop and thinks, "I'm sorry. I am sorry. We are making acts of blind faith." She sends out a text across the ocean and into her future and the man in the phone's future, to a time when she will be asleep and he will be awake. She writes him. *I hope you slept well.*

Sometimes they have sex through the Whatsapp video feature. When they do, she is extra aware of the lighting and contortions of her face. Most of the sex happens off screen. The limiting nature of the cell phone camera that calms her by confining their relationship to a face and small amounts of now-familiar living room background, works against physical intimacy. She has no desire to see his body compartmentalized into segments, the chest, the genitals, an awkward angle of his ass and lower back. He does not ask her to show him her body and she does not volunteer. Always, as she works to hold the camera at a flattering angle, she worries just a tiny bit that he might be recording, not because she thinks he would but because he could, might upload her, moaning and sighing, to some site that she will never find out about and would it be worse to be there without knowing? And who is this guy, anyway? He says perfect things to her and they both always come hard. She imagines, each time, moon colored people spilling out of her, tubby, satisfying balls like amoebas, sometimes with legs, as if morphing into the next phase of life, sometimes encased in gooey mucus, heads breaking through to gasp clear air, sometimes they dance out, slick as if in the rain, leaping low and delighting in gravity and she thinks, before she comes, "The moon at the spoon spoon color," though she has no idea why. She does not tell the man in the phone about the amoeba people. She does not tell him about Greg Smith.

If they meet in person, she thinks, it will be awkward. Each of them with whole and full-sized bodies, lumpy and constant.

In her first email Celeste had spoken of, *The weight of what is in our lives that is beautiful.* She said, *In your home you will see all the things that are memories of your life, memories from people, memories you collect. These memories, is it freedom?* The email continued to discuss the unnecessary weight of wealth and insinuate the relief of freeing oneself from that burden, and reading, it was clear to Lanna that Celeste was not being poetic, not imagining a home crowded with the memories, nostalgia laying all over the floor to be tripped on, the last time you saw that friend, your aunt's smile at your graduation. Rather Celeste comes from a language where objects, once they gain a certain age, are called memories, are, themselves, memories.

When Lanna read that, *memories of your life*, she wanted to smash all the chachkies and souvenirs in her apartment and she knew that if she did she would then immediately, upon smashing them, cuddle them to her, all the shards and fragments and torn up bits, and dust them off her chest into boxes that she would open a few times a year, dragging her hands through the debris while her stomach clenched and ached, boxes she would move every time she changed apartments. Boxes she might someday have to explain to someone, why do we keep moving the boxes of broken things, they might ask. It was easier to explain a plastic napkin ring—Amanda and I stole those from a restaurant once, when we were not going to see each other for a long time, and we each have one—than shards of a napkin ring in a box.

She can love the man in the phone through the winter and through the long, dark spring, she knows, but she does not know if she will love him in the summer, green and easy, when you can leave the house in shorts, a thin dress, be out the door in a few breaths. When she thinks this she clutches at her phone, opens WhatsApp to re-read the last messages he sent.

Celeste's first email ended this way, *I discovered your identity that intrigued me to drop you a line. Let now seize this moment and start to be acquainted. Together I am sure that we enjoy a great life so cold and hot and beyond. Respectfully, Celeste.* Lanna has house slippers she got from the impulse-buy section at Walgreens. They are furry pink pigs, with floppy ears and big round eyes look up at her when she walks. One day she has her feet up on the table, laptop against her thighs, and she leans the pink pig snouts towards each other and makes kissing noises, a puppet joke for herself. The pigs cuddle, more convincingly than she expected, and she feels a wave of loneliness and yanks her feet apart. "Yeah," she says to the pigs that look back at her. "So?"

For months she has had terrible periods. Since the winter has begun. Since she returned from her vacation. The thought of going to the doctor, the layers of her clothing, long underwear and wool socks and hats and scarves, piled on an office chair while she shivers under a paper gown, exhausts her when she is on her period and, as soon as it stops each month, she thinks, "It wasn't that bad." She worries, while it is happening, that she might disappear out of her uterus. Not metaphorically, not that her sense of self will disappear into a child born of her womb, into a reproduction of herself that will live independently, that will stand and walk and dig holes and taste leaves and then, in turn, disappear into a reproduction of herself. She worries that, in fluid and chunks of flesh, she will empty out and become, bit by bit, nothing knowable or reproduced in the world. She wonders what the man in the phone would think if he knew about how terrible her periods were.

She says, "I'm a bit tired today. I have my period."

He says, "If I was there I'd rub your back."

She says, "Show me your hands."

He holds up the hand that is not holding the phone so that, except the constant rectangle of herself, she sees nothing other than his hand on the screen, and she knows that her brain does some unfelt action to transform the flat image into something muscled and correctly sized.

She imagines him rubbing her back and sighs. She imagines him rubbing her back and feels his hands pushing, dissolving her to disappear out more quickly. She thinks that she should call the man in the phone even though she is talking to the man in the phone.

When he hangs up and she stops seeing him in her phone she puts it down and emails a few more Greg Smiths.

Every day she comes home and goes into the bathroom, the warmest place, and opens her email and her WhatsApp, hovering as close as she can to the hot steel loops of the radiator. Occasionally she sways a little and touches the metal and burns her skin. After six weeks of emailing Greg Smiths, checking her inbox has become habit, action without expectation, though she knows that there must be some expectation because she feels disappointed each time there are no messages from Greg Smith.

For two weeks the home of the man in the phone becomes infested with ants. It is nice to think about a place where winter is warm enough for ants. He spends most of their calls wandering his apartment, looking down at the floor, dropping occasionally to wipe scent trails with vinegar and Lanna mostly sees the top of his head, the phone held inattentively and shaky. It is intriguing to know that, away across the ocean, they battle ants the same way. She grows lax about the lighting on her own image. By the time his borax traps start to work she is not sure she is in love, not sure she wants to look at him through the phone anymore.

Two months in she still finds more Greg Smiths to email and she is amazed. Some days she maintains very clear records, spreadsheets with dates and addresses and an empty *responses* column. Some days she finds addresses and cuts and pastes and does not care that she might cut and paste the same address again later. .org, .edu, .com, .net. She knows she might be emailing the same Greg Smiths again and again, Greg Smith at different moments in his life. Greg Smith in college and a first job and a volunteer position and hiding purchases from his girlfriend, each Greg Smith fractured into dozens, and she, reaching back across time, through the strata of every Greg Smith, grieves that not one segment, not one layer of one Greg Smith, will respond.

Though she now feels an unsteady ambivalence towards loving the man in the phone, she tells him again and again how to hook her, how to get her to fall into a clear love with him.

"Text me when you get out of the shower," she says. He arches his eyebrows, and she says, "It's not sex. It's not sexy like that you are naked. It's sexy like the clean smell of soap. And the warm and humidness. While it's such dry winter here."

He does not seem to understand that she has given up the secret to her love and she feels relieved even as she is hurt and frustrated.

"Sing me a lullaby," she says, and he laughs and changes the subject.

Day later he sends her a voice memo, him singing a gentle song in his language with a waltz rhythm and she falls sound asleep, pillows cuddled in her arms and spooned up against her back.

She wakes after a profound rest to a picture of a smiley face drawn on a mirror in after-shower steam. It makes her feel rage and she does not know why.

At Walgreens she discovers that they keep antacids under lock and key. She wanders aisles till she finds an employee, a young man, and peers at his nametag to see if it might say Greg. It does not. He reaches for a white service phone and her stomach clenches more tightly. His voice, "Customer service, customer service needed in the antacid aisle," echoes through the store. "I don't have a key," he explains.

Almost daily she looks at her darkened phone screen and aches. Everything outside so dead, the trees and grass and the man so far away and never fully satisfying. She feels herself a new and future species swimming blind through the pulling tides of cold oceans, dispersed and unconnected, until he calls and she answers and comes to anchor, clutching the phone, inside her phone, realized there and more and more permanent each time. "I am becoming cyber coral," she thinks. She will say this to the man in the phone if he calls. If he finds it clever she will be pleased. She swears to never call him again or at least not for a few days. She calls him before he goes to bed.

She emails at Greg Smith out of habit, gritting her teeth and demanding blind faith, and then she is home with a cold for two days and the sun shines brilliantly and, once again, she feels that he might, indeed, return her email and there might, indeed, be something about Money Power Love and she panics that he, her Greg Smith, the one that responds, could be the kind of man who likes to roughhouse with little kids under the pretense of having a good time, being a cool uncle but, actually, pins kids to the floor to feel strong and powerful. She takes deep breaths and thinks that continuing to send emails when Greg Smith could be an ugly person, must be blind faith. And she thinks that this man, this man who pushes little children, he above all others might need things about love and power and maybe even money.

On a Monday in late January she watches *Antiques Roadshow* and begins to have nightmares. Too many old woes come through the TV, out of the eyes of dolls and painted-over trousseaux. They are standard nightmares, casual breaking and enterings, people grabbing her. In the cold dark of her bedroom she wakes terrified and also with a musty feel, like she needs to be aired in the sun. She holds her phone for a while and then calls the man in her phone, living in an old, old city across the sea in tomorrow's daylight and, when he answers, her face, reflecting the blue light of her phone, a ghost shadow up in the corner of the screen, she says, "Take me out onto the street and show me that old, old city in use."

The email, she guesstimates, has gone out to twenty-five hundred Greg Smiths. She finds a new email address and writes:

> Greg Smith, At my closest coffee shop, no matter what time I get there, I am the only customer and once I got a coffee for there and it came in a plastic mug that was supposed to look like glass, but it had those cracks through it that old plastic gets. Today someone had taped a sign on the tip jar. This:

> Tips are like hugs but without the awkward body contact.

> I put twenty dollars in. I will never return. I felt heavy, Greg Smith.

Then she copies and pastes the regular email below, starting with the sentence, *There could be something in this.* She types *Come on Greg Smith* in the subject line and sends. She sends this email to four more Greg Smiths.

Later the man in the phone calls and she says, "Describe what it feels like to touch my skin." He holds up a hand to the camera, the skin grey and out of focus in the light of his apartment. The lines on his palms cast some of the skin a darker grey.

He says, "Soft. Perfect."

She says, "Do you remember?"

He says, "Yes."

She says, "You too."

She does not remember. The only skin she can really remember is the cheeks of a friend's baby she visited a few days before. That skin is still specific.

She has one house plant and it clings to life. Watering it is an act of anxiety and joy. She loves the heady power of providing it life and worries that she will over or under water it, that she will wake up and its few leaves will be fallen to the earth and she will not know how, through excess or deprivation, she killed the plant. One day, as she glugs water into the pot, enough that it seeps out into the dish below, as instructed by an indoor gardener website, she sees, laying on the soil, a lone, round, pale bloated thing that is not soil. She thinks perhaps it is a seed come awash to the top of the dirt, ready to germinate, or perhaps the egg of a bug or a small rock. She picks it up and squeezes. It ruptures and a spray of cool thin liquid wets her hand.

Two days in a row, at work, once while listening to a presentation and once while sitting in her cubicle, she feels she might be bleeding. Not menstrual bleeding but bleeding from under her breast and the creases in her elbows. Lanna knows it is probably sweat, still, she goes to the bathroom and lifts up her shirt and she is not bleeding. The way that it feels like she is bleeding from under her breast is more like it is related to her bra underwire than a stigmata feeling. She does not know why she thinks that. She does not know how she knows the word *stigmata* and she does not know if the bleeding on the sides is called a stigmata or just the palms.

The second time it happens she raises up her shirt and looks at her unbloodied torso in the bathroom mirror and thinks about how she didn't yet look up exactly what a stigmata is. She thinks that the marks on the chest are from the spears of Romans and she does not know how she knows this and wonders if she might be becoming a saint. Would she have to go to a church regularly to become a saint? She wonders if you hallucinate when you are crucified. It upsets her, standing in the bathroom at work with so much skin showing, how delightful she finds the word crucified, just as a collection of sounds. She cannot connect the sounds to the act of murder or to feelings about the act of murder.

"At least I am not bleeding," she thinks. She wonders if there was a time when people really did not understand about the uterine lining. What a thing to be a little girl and just begin to bleed. And rabbits. She had read an article about how, for a while and maybe still in some places, if you missed periods, you could inject a rabbit with your pee and then, bamb, bamb, kill the rabbit to look if its ovaries had gone funny and know if you were pregnant or just not bleeding. She wondered how people knew that pee would do it. She wondered if the rabbits got eaten. If women ate their rabbits.

Celeste sends an email. The first in months. The subject line is a series of hearts and kissy lips. Lanna does not open it, afraid Celeste has streamlined her offerings, no longer hawking Power or Money but only Love. Lanna does not want to edit her Greg Smith email. She does not want to know only about Love.

There is a day of unexpected warmth. The sunshine is not so cold and people are out in only sweaters.

"What if I came to see you?" she asks the man in the phone.

He closes his eyes and there is a long pause.

He says, "I would be very happy."

"It would be hard," she says, thinking of his wholeness and his moving of his own volition.

"We would be happy," he says.

"You would be whole and move about of your own volition."

"We would be happy," he says.

It makes her angry, the simpleness of his answer, this whole and constant human who would wake and sleep at the same time she did. Also she knows that if she goes across the ocean simple things might wow her, stuff like grocery stores and monuments, dime a dozen things to a native but, to someone from far away, great. A way to be unafraid. To be wide-eyed and proud. After she ends the call and her phone screen goes dark, she whispers, "Greg Smith. Greg Smith. I believe that if you answer the email you could be granted such enthusiasms for the world."

She remembers hearing about a man who met a woman one time and then, when he could not find her again, mass emailed as many people as he could find with her name. The woman never got back to him, but everyone with the same name emailed each other and started a club and then a charitable foundation. In the To: field on a new email, Lanna types *g* and then adds all the Greg Smith emails that pop down. Then she types *s*. Then *gr. gs*. She works her way through the alphabet. She adds and adds emails and perhaps they are the same twenty emails again and again or perhaps they are hundreds of Greg Smiths. Thousands.

Subject: Greg Smith You Are Greg Smith

Come on, Greg Smith. Come on. None of you responded to the possibility of knowing or finding or having Money/Power/Love. You are all full up? Don't want more? But I really expected one of you to do it but we will never know what is beyond the veil of Celeste. Not one of you. Now I give you this instead: other Greg Smiths. You are all here together on this email and together you can find things about Money/Power/Love and I believe that. Because you are more together. When you do find something, please, one of you, remember and let me know: What did you learn? I'm not bccing you. That would be the correct thing for privacy. I found these addresses through internet searches anyway and this is a moment of blind faith so sorry about the privacy. I want you to know each other. Make a fire Greg Smith. Build the fire of the passion of Greg Smith.

Best,
Lanna

At the check-in counter the customer service provider says, "Your gate will change. Your gate is B47."

"What?" says Lanna.

"Have a nice day," says the customer service woman.

"OK," says Lanna.

She sits at the gate for an hour, on edge, expecting to look up and see the screen behind the airline agent suddenly displaying a different destination. The boarding area overflows, and a middle-aged man sits on the floor, cross legged, with his back to the outside window. Ten minutes before boarding, he says, "I dominated that pizza." He travels alone and no one acknowledges his statement and Lanna only looks at him out of the side of her eyes. When he clambers up off the carpet to get in line, she sees he has left a pizza box leaned dramatically and intentionally against the steel girder window support. It is a trophy and a warning signal.

She thinks about how once she dated a man who liked to breath loudly into her ear, long slow, heavy breaths. He said, "Uhhhhhhhh," into her ear, and it sounded as if he were dying dramatically. No matter how many times she pulled her head away, trying to indicate her dislike, he insisted on doing it. It was his move. "Uhhhhhhhh." It made her feel claimed and alone. It made her feel, for brief moments, like she was clutching a long suffering and unpleasant victim of a hip fracture. She guessed that he wanted her to do the same thing to him, but she was too selfish to comply. The man in the phone, when they are together, perhaps he will want to groan like this in her ear.

She feels the rubbery skin that covers her phone so that it is less likely to break when it slips from her hands. When she drops it. She wants to WhatsApp the man in her phone, to have him there on the screen, to protect her from this fear about him. There is no time to call. She is in line and then showing the boarding pass on her phone, still worried that she is entering the wrong flight, and she is scrambling up the jetway, dragging her carry-on behind.

The safety announcements come first in that other language she has failed to acquire. Then the flight attendants translate instructions into imperfect English. The flight attendants say, "Guide strips will illuminate in darkness." They speak about flotation and breathing and safety belts and oxygen. They say, "When your electronic device gets hot, has sparks and smoking, please unplug your device and alert a member of the cabin crew."

"When," repeats Lanna.

They rise from the earth and the cabin lights dim and rows and rows of passengers drape themselves in red airplane blankets as if all prepared to take part in a religious ceremony and she is shivering and stands and grabs at the backs of seats and stumbles to the lavatory through the resting penitents.

IT WILL TAKE THE VILLAGE:
THE 24/7 THIS IS YOUR BODY WAY! YES!

It will be thirty-one months since I auditioned, since I came to demonstrate my abilities. Room and board and full medical and a small salary in exchange for the tomatoes. That was the deal. But I knew at once it was not for the tomatoes. I was not to be compensated for the tomatoes, but for devotion to him. To the critical project of him. We are all quiet. Quiet men. All of us working here with the vegetables and grains and meats. If you come close, though, you feel how we thrum. To be a part of something unknown. His project that he has undertaken. A human body manipulated to perfection. His human body being made perfect. Made to last in perfection.

We curate. We nurse. We guard. We build. We understand the possibility. We take it to the next level.

I cannot falter.

I am with the tomatoes. I am the tomato man. I am the tomato man. I have made the other tomato men superfluous. A burden on the vine. They were cut. Paul, for example, is a cucumber man. I never could be. Such a hard and untelling fruit. He doesn't think so, I suppose. And the carrots and the peas. Each man correct for their specific produce. We cannot deny the rightness of our specific produce. I am a tomato man.

I am with the tomatoes. When the moment arrives I know. The prickly smell a bit sweeter. The color flush and regular. The vine leans almost imperceptibly. *Here. I have made this.*

Cupped in the palm.

Take it now.
And I do.

Once. Once it was in a night rain. A warm, late-summer night, when all the tomatoes have a blush that indicates hours or minutes before they finish, the time when I rarely sleep, only occasional naps when the temperature dips enough to stop the ripening, naps out in the furrows just before dawn. And I jerk awake when the heat rises above 63 degrees and the tomatoes sugar again.

But, once, the evening still warm and the rain had begun and through the smell of wet earth I breathed that scent of perfect change.

In the darkness, with my nose and my fingers, I hunted out the tomato, the ready tomato. Firm and soft. Newly sweet. And I harvested it, a twist, the vine giving way, releasing the fruit.

I crept to his bedroom. Knocked at the door.

"A tomato is ready," I said.

He shuffled around in the sheets and opened the door. I knew that if I could see his face it would be sleep lined and serious and focused.

He took the tomato from me and ate it. I thought of him drinking the rain from the tomato's skin before he bit the fruit.

When he finished he said, "Thank you," and closed the door.

I had not wiped clean the surface of this tomato. And so he drank the rain and ate the little grit of soil from the taught skin of that exactly finished tomato.

I think of that tomato often.

He takes no pleasure in the consumption. It is only for his health. So I pleasure in his consumption. The tomato deserves that.

Once there was a rumor, whispered among the furrows, that he would quit tomatoes. Publications had started to question the acidity and Jaime, a radish man who has a connection to the phlebot-omist's cousin, said that vitamin C levels had been high several weeks in a row and that some research linked gastroesophageal dyspepsia and tomatoes. And for weeks, until counter data was released and he introduced teff to his diet and the creases left his brow, I quietly decreased his tomato intake. I only brought the loveliest. The most red. The most plump and modeled heirlooms. Eventually the rumor stopped because nothing happened. I will never know if there was actually hesitation as he took the tomatoes from the unbleached jute cloth. If the tomatoes were in peril. My job.

Exact times are crucial. The second of completion. The second of picking. Each of us, the cucumber men, the pea men, the kohlrabi, the frisée, we have a constant calculation running in our heads as we rush to find him with our ripe harvest. The temperature. The rate of degradation of our particular produce. Very occasionally I arrive at the same moment as another grower man and we murmur to each other a number, a percent. .00003176. .000294. The smaller number steps aside to ensure that he ingests the least decay.

After slow, methodical chewing, incisors, molars, incisors, molars and the whole food is gone and he breaths deep into his diaphragm and then breaths deep again and exhales, he-ha-he-ha, several small thrusts of air, and he performs a Hindi abdominal rub, then, if one of us remains, he looks to the harvest that still waits in our hands in an unbleached jute cloth. We say a number and if it is greater than .0004 he will shake his head and the harvest shall be composted. Similarly, while he is consuming our produce we continue to calculate and we may mummer *.0004*, indicating that so much time has elapsed that the fruit is decayed beyond .0004%. He will finish his incisor, molar, incisor, molar chewing and replace what is left of the harvest into the unbleached jute cloth and the remains shall be composted.

He smells of garden.

I ate at Arby's.

I had forgotten that until I woke up from a dream of it here in the tomatoes.

Not forgotten. Repressed. Did not allow the memory. But there I was. In the tomato bed. With my dream of Arby's. I defiled the tomatoes with my dream and with the sweat from my sleeping body that must have seeped into the earth. Sweat made of Arby's.

And what I found out in this dream is that I would go again. I would go to Arby's again.

The chicken meat pressed round and fried. The airy, thin bread. The meaningless, pale slice of tomato.

It happened while he was on Solstice Fast. Winter Solstice Fast that goes forever and ever. He is gone and the tomatoes are quiet. It is a time to finger aerate the soil and calibrate the nitrates and the phosphates and taste the earth for alkalinity and to run the mineralized river water through the unbleached jute clothes.

And I went to Arby's and I ate.

I would be sent away if he knew. I should be sent away.

I have forgotten what my body looks like. I have a sense of its weight against the earth between the rows of tomatoes. I know the size of my fingers against the tomatoes. But I do not perceive my body. After so many years I only perceive his body. His forearm thickness. The muscle density and specific oxygenation of blood. He does not burden us with the information. Our job is to do our job. But there are tells. A certain wrinkle in the brow after the phlebotomist comes. Mitch will shave him twice in one day and we know that shaving calms him. From this we know that the data was not good. Levels too high or low. I must be clam in these moments or I will grasp the tomatoes too roughly, cortisol will leak from me and infect the plants.

There are rice men and millet men. I sometimes pass them slushing about in their puddles and fields. I could not understand them. I can understand Paul, a cucumber man. I could not be a cucumber man, but I understand. Grains that go so far from themselves to him—threshing and boiling—I cannot understand a quinoa man.

Each tomato has an average of 22 calories. We get a more exact guesstimate on each tomato via the scales that are all around the house and the grounds. When I arrive with a tomato he steps on the nearest scale and then steps on it again after eating. He says, "tomato," and the system calculates the probable calories, taking into account a standard ratio between water weight and the flesh of a tomato. And so with the rice. With rabbit. With all the foods. All day Robert, the scale man, circles the grounds, perfecting, perfecting the calibrations on each scale.

At the end of the quarter the system adds together the calories and, based on what we call the "lean consumption", perfection based on correct deprivation, a 1,637 calorie-a-day diet, determines how much he has over-consumed and, thus, determines the fast days. Because of this, after the opulence and wealth of the late fall, the Winter Solstice Fast is long, long, long.

There are 600 calories in the King's Hawaiian Roast Beef and Swiss Sandwich.

I don't know where the meat comes from in the Crispy Chicken Sandwich. It tastes mostly of something like salt.

My dream that made me remember. When I woke I wept with pleasure and shame.

At the Spring Equinox Fast I returned. As I knew I would. As I tried to believe I would not. I ate the Angus Three Cheese and Bacon Sandwich.

Days later I forced myself to purge. At night. In secret. In silence.

All the other tomato men were let go because they slipped up. The tomatoes too early, too late. Forgotten. Concentration broken. And they were not needed. We were 12 hours on 12 hours off and now I am 24 hours on.

At Summer Solstice the harvest had already been so plentiful, the grains in early, the vines heavy, the beds of greens bushy and over on the far side, where I never go, over the hill and into the meadows, two ostrich and a bison had reached optimal muscle density during that quarter so he had eaten and eaten and there were many fast days.

By the third day of sitting with the tomatoes and pulling the fruit to go straight into the compost, by the third night laid down in my bed of vines, my skin alert to the temperatures, to the moments when the fruits might rest, pause in the metamorphosis to ripe, I rose up and quietly I snuck. I snuck. There is no other word for it. I snuck to Arby's. I had Aunt Annie's™ Cheddar Pretzel Nuggets and a Smoke House Brisket. I let the juices be on my chin and down into the crevices of my fingers. Yellow mustard under my nails. When I left I only regretted that I had not opened the bun and rubbed it against my hair. My neck. The sauce. The next day I regretted all. And I slept. And when I woke I took one of his tomatoes. One of my wards. I grasped it and twisted at the moment of ripe and ran, ran, ran to the car, blowing stop lights, swerving, .000937, to Arby's. I sliced it and, .00215, placed it on the Roast Beef Classic, nestled between the meat and bun, the saggy, damp lettuce blanketing the tomato like a clinging, needed death, and I ate. And the tomato was defiled and glorious.

I am the tomato man. I am all that is needed.

The fast is over and I must only think of the tomato. Of transferring the tomato from the vine to his body at the exact moment. Exact.

I must not think of the Arby-Q.

Before there was nothing to rival the tomato. The tomato that he would consume. Now, I find, the Orange Cream Shake and the Horse

Radish Spread sing, yes sing, in discord to the tomato. My nose feels undelicate. The earth and the plant less nuanced.

He will not suffer for my desires. After so long, after these years, I cannot lose focus.

That first time, that first time at the Arby's, I had gone to look at some tomato varieties, new heirlooms that produced increased levels of foliate and lycopene. On the way home I needed to use the restroom. That most natural and most perverse thing we do. The only place for miles around, an Arby's at the corner of two country roads. I went in, after so many years in the tomatoes, and the smell and the light, greasy-sweet and bright, like screaming in my nose and eyes and I stumbled to the bathroom and that is when I realized that I did not perceive my own body. I stood in front of the mirror and raised up my hands and watched the reflection. It was like I manipulated a ghost. And when I left the bathroom, big door swung wide, I did not smell the smell of Arby's anymore, my olfactory nerves accustomed and at rest, and the light was not so harsh and I knew about stepping up, about ordering, about saying, "number 3," and, "large," and about extra ketchup packets. And I did all these things.

Now I shiver. I force my eyes to meet his. I am pale. I feel pale. Like the bun. Like the roast turkey. Like the potato cakes. I am the potato cakes. I worry that he might lick me like I lick the earth and taste the potato cake. He does not lick us. But I stand ready to evade him, just in case, when I bring the tomatoes. And once I let the percent go beyond .0004 because I am thinking about how he knows that I am thinking about a Cherry Turnover. I yell, "Stop!" No murmur. A yell. A yell. I hold out the unbleached jute cloth and if I let him see my eyes he would see pleading. For forgiveness. Forgiveness. I back out of the room and cannot stop my thoughts from going to Roast Beef. I will be sent away. I cannot be sent away. I am a tomato man. I am the tomato man. I am his tomato man. I am here for his project, for his body that, through exquisite curation of consumption, is a new possibility.

He has gone. I came with the tomato and he has gone.

I have read the blogs.

To live on a boat. A marine diet. He. And an MRI machine and a radiologist. Weekly brain scans and a fisherman and he will pluck everything from the ocean—the fishes and the seaweed and the clams—and he will eat it all alive, the fishes gasping for water and the seaweed still anchored to the rocks.

This is the key to health. The studies show. This is right consumption. I think of the tomato plucked in the night rain. The night rain on his tongue and in his blood.

A letter arrived for each of us. We are all let go. We have two weeks to find housing. Other food.

I have done something. With paper and pen. I wrote to Arby's asking them to consider a valued customer punch card. I would enjoy it more if I ate in anticipation of my tenth meal free.

I have not left yet. I am alone in my furrow. The tomatoes sag around me, yearning for the earth where their fruit and seed will molder and hatch into new life.

The letter to Arby's is now in my lap and the house empty of him and his health and muscle density. The car is still here. I could drive. To Arby's. Out into the world away from the grounds and the draining rice patties and the bellows of bison loaded into trucks. I don't. I don't go.

With my fingers I separate tiny green suckers from the forks in the tomato vines. I crush the stems and leaves in my hand and breath the green, green pungent scent and I lay on the earth and fan out my legs and arms. They rip the tomato vines. I feel about for the letter to Arby's that has slid to the earth and I hold it in my hands and I feed it into my mouth, slowly, saliva dampening and degenerating the paper until I can roll the pulp around in my mouth, tear it apart with my tongue, and then I swallow.

MY WALPHARM FAMILY

I was supposed to write these case notes every day. The non-profit Life's All Services Focused for This Community's Continuing Change's (LASFCCC) Employment Training Program (ETP) wanted me to spend an hour after all the clients went home and today Martha made progress on her resume and Jeanine stocked the canned goods and forgot to go oldest to newest and Phil wrote obscenities on the table about his cock and someone's tits but at least he did it while wearing his WalPharm blue. But fuck that. Every day I smoked a few cigarettes and ate a tube of Oreos and it was time to get the hell out of that faux WalPharm and then when I had to submit end-of-training evals I locked the Supervisor Room door all day like fuck off, the door's locked, and made up shit about the last three months, scribbled in different colored pens so it looked legit, and when I busted out for a smoke they were all what should I do and I shouted inventory aisle seven or try and buy some Icy Hot No Mess Vapor Gel. I don't care that it's not a Shoppy Day. Always be prepared. Always. Remember our motto. Always be prepared.

It would be hard when the Oreos were gone.

Don't get me wrong. They could all fucking do the shit. They worked. We worked. They filled out applications and interviewed and did checkout. But those case notes just fucking killed me. Under such minute scrutiny anything real couldn't hold up. True things dissolved.

I unlocked the doors of our donated WalPharm that is a great tax write-off for WalPharm, dropped my stuff in the Supervisor Room and sat cross-legged up on one of the check-out counters reading a People. Over the past two years I'd read all the magazines, Cosmo and The Enquirer and Ladies' Home Journal and everything, three times and was on my fourth go-round and I didn't have to work hard to forget Monica Lewinsky's blowjobs and the spring fashion was fresh again and the Newsweeks had the Y2K cover that freaked me out because we were actually getting close now. I left those Newsweeks alone and just relearned new sex positions and considered sending the info along to Monica and tried to figure out my season and how to shave chocolate. I'd grabbed a Be Mine aluminum foil balloon on a plastic stick and tapped it against my head while I read about Diana's Legacy of Love. There are candy hearts and a bin of red lace garters and specialty You Light Me Up cigars in the front. I guess it had been coming up on Valentine's Day when this WalPharm went under and the company left all the merchandise to the training program so it was Valentine's Day everyday with us and the balloons had only deflated a little.

DiAngelo was in first. He was always first or last, bright and showing off his blue or black ballpoint pen, ready to work, or with the rims of his eyes red and shit, man, why do we got to do this shit again?

"How you doing, DiAngelo?" I asked.

"Bianca, I'm looking sharp," he said. That's what he said every day, even on the days when he came all late and pissed off.

DiAngelo was about fifty. I had everyone's data but I never remembered exactly. That day he swaggered in with a purple suit, green shirt and the tie orange. He always wore solid colors and a black fedora with a silver band that said DiAngelo in curvy metal letters around the front and he would not wear a cotton-polyester-blend WalPharm shirt and I wouldn't have either if I looked so fucking sharp.

"How are you this morning, Miss Thing?" he said.

"Keeping on. Keeping on." I took a pull from my travel mug.

"Gonna get nasty out there. That's what the weatherman said and look at those clouds. You think I can get one of these cigars?"

I shrugged.

I got told all the time that the stuff in the store was for training purposes only but, I mean, it had been rotting on the shelves twenty-some months and we were supposed to be helping people and anyway the trainees didn't usually ask and when they did they came up and said real quiet my kid's coming to visit and I want something nice or I'm meeting my parole officer and I want my nails to look good. What's our motto? Always be prepared. That is what I said to them because I couldn't say your shame is so fucking unnecessary.

DiAngelo put the cigar in his pocket and grabbed a tiny chocolate heart. He looked at me to make sure that was okay.

"Got something special tonight?"

"Might do." He leaned back on the heels of his shoes, black with white saddles.

"You treat the ladies right," I said.

"Took me too long to learn. Well. Big day in here."

"Shoppy Day." Some days I divided the trainees into shoppers and workers and set them loose in our abandoned WalPharm. We called it Shoppy Day. They called it something else in the original employee training pilot project in Oklahoma and, nationwide, all successful models have Shoppy Day or whatever components. I'm supposed to take photos for our grantors.

DiAngelo said, "This is the job, man. I'm gonna get this job. I could really use this job, Miss Thing."

I think that DiAngelo has done some real bad shit.

The little bus from Our Village of Our Hope pulled up and DiAngelo went back to the Teaching Room.

Good-morning, Good-morning Miss Bianca it's Shoppy Day. Bianca there is going to be a storm. Shoppy Day.

The Our Village of Our Hopers loved to shuffle through the sliding door one by one, everyone waiting for the door to shut behind the person in front of them. Swish ding. Swish ding. Swish ding. My turn. My turn. You're supposed to go after me. Wait for the door. Swish ding.

Cathy stopped short.

"Fuck," I said to myself.

"One is missing." She pointed to the display box of tiny chocolate hearts. Cathy had rearranged the Valentine's display the day before and she remembered details and it was amazing because if the entire

Household Cleaners section disappeared it would have taken me weeks to notice but she saw this tiny heart out of place and it was so fucking annoying. I had to save all the Oreo tube containers and stuff them with Kleenex and put them back on the shelves. Cathy really liked rules.

"Cathy. Good job. You noticed," I said.

"The heart."

"I'll put it back later. I was testing you."

"That's not nice, Miss Bianca," said Les. Les had a crush on Cathy.

"Go on back. Les. Everyone. What's our motto?"

"Always be prepared."

"Right."

Cathy had somehow found out that Life's All Services Focused for This Community's Continuing Change wanted me to keep the door locked all the time, I guess to keep people from wandering in, but I never locked the door because the WalPharm was in the middle of a bunch of vacant warehouses. In the beginning I worried that former customers might come but then I remembered that the WalPharm had shut down because they had no customers and on the first day of each training I taught rule one, when you are at work, stay at work. Anyway, it scared me, locking us in. Cathy hovered by the door all the time, um, I think this is supposed to be locked. Miss Bianca. Locked. I made the mistake of saying that I was afraid of fire that's why it's unlocked. She started hovering in the sliding doorway when I smoked, ding, ding, ding, you are too close to the building. What if the wind comes and blows your cigarette out of your hand? I wanted to kill her so I was glad that, at least, it hadn't been the fucking door that morning.

We straggled back to the Teaching Room. The Teaching Room still had the engraved Employee Lounge sign on the door and an Employee of the Month plaque adhered to the far wall and Todd Ramos, his name on a slip of paper and his WalPharm printed photo slotted behind squares of plastic on the plaque, had reigned as Employee of the Month since WalPharm gave up the building. Todd Ramos with his curly blond hair.

Shoppy Day, so everyone looked good in case they pulled Shopper. Elvira sported her gold-lamé skirt and Keisha's hair was done and the red lettering stood out really fucking crisp against the black on Roy's Bulls jersey.

In each three-month training I only did four Shoppy Days, and all the clients got so pumped about what they were going to pull, customer or stock or whatever, that the morning-skills session was shot. I usually just ran a movie but to be honest I thought I might go at the Pain Relief shelves to see how fast one could incur fatal stomach bleeding from ibuprofen intake if I had to watch *The WalPharm Family: Employees, Employers and Customers together in the Circle that Sustains* one more time. That's a fucking triangle. Not a circle. And the whole *Keys to Your Future: Unlocking Success in the World of Jobs* series. Christ. On those days I made sure I brought an extra travel mug and I took a swig every time there was a firm handshake during the *Building Relationships with Your Co-Workers* installment and with the applications episode it was when the voiceover said with your blue or black ballpoint pen, and for all of them I drank a couple big swallows whenever I heard this is the key that fits.

There were eighteen in this group and half of them showed up together on a little bus from Our Village of Our Hope and the other half were from GED To Great Employee Development and came like I did on public transit. The GEDers had all got paroled early because, I guess, they promised to want to be great employees and, if they made it through, WalPharm might ignore their criminal backgrounds and give them a job. So we all worked together, the former convicts and the disabled and me. They graduated and went on to jobs and I stayed in the fake WalPharm. And this group fucking bickered all the time and so I had rolled through the movies to shut them up but we had a month left.

The Hopers were already buzzed about graduation so I just let them talk about it for the entire M-skills. Our Village of Our Hope insisted we run an actual graduation for their people each session, a few balloons in the Teaching Room and certificates and families come. It is a pain in my ass to have to be in on a Saturday but it is really fucking sweet because, every time so far, the graduates walked up and shook hands and we talked about what they had learned and when I was about to fall over dead from boredom it all broke down into the friends the families and all the students hugging each other. And they give me a card signed by everyone with a five-dollar coupon to WalPharm. So real sweet and I had all those cards and coupons in my desk in the Supervisor Room because I could never go into a real WalPharm. The idea scared the shit out of me.

"What about graduation?" I said and the Hopers galloped away talking about decorations and certificates and other people got out a deck of cards and Roy drew on the table and Keisha opened her cellular telephone that she was so proud to be the only one of us to have a cell but she could never get reception so just flipped it open and closed and open and closed and I spaced out and nursed my travel mug and wondered if we should move the shoe polish over by Cosmetics.

In the middle of all the graduation chatter, to no one in particular, DiAngelo said, "I'm bringing my daughter."

We all turned to look at him and he pulled his hat forward on his head. Usually a few days before we finished up and when the trainees from Our Village of Our Hope had been talking and talking about it for the whole three months a staff person got off the little bus when it came for pick up and stood a few feet in from the sliding door and said to the linoleum that there would be a graduation on Saturday and seats were limited and so to tell me now if you were coming and you could invite one person and the Hopers said yes, yes me and the staff person smiled at them. The GEDers didn't come.

"You gonna come to their graduation?" said Keisha.

"Their graduation? It's our graduation," said DiAngelo

"Are you kidding me? Get the fuck out of here and get a job, man."

"We are doing something here. It's part of the journey. You gotta honor that kind of thing."

"Fuck off," said Keisha.

"Oh. That will be nice," said Les. When we talked about savings goals Les said that he would save for a hat with his name written on a band. He called it a hat belt and he wanted the letters to be pink. He also wanted to buy a hat belt for Cathy, but he only told me that.

When we took a five-minute break lots of the GEDers came out and smoked with me. The sky had turned black and the wind screamed so we hunched around our cigarettes.

"You got a daughter, Di?" I shouted over the wind.

"Got a bunch. I got one I think will talk to me."

Early Shift/Cashier was the Shoppy Day big deal. A lot of places for people to fail, but if they pulled it off they were the hero here at our WalPharm and at the end of Shoppy Day when I let everyone open one bottle of purple or red Wyler's Light Drink they toasted the Early Shift/Cashiers. Ready for the big time. Always be prepared they said.

We didn't ever touch the Minute Made orange juice from concentrate or anything in the refrigerator because that shit had got to be rank after so long. But the Wyler's Light had seven years till the expiration date. Twist cap to open. Water. Maltodextrin. Aspartame. Consider refrigeration after seal is broken.

I chose DiAngelo and Cathy because I thought Di was ready and Cathy drove me crazy on Shoppy Days telling the Early Shift/Cashiers what to do so I figured she could just be out on the floor. Everyone else cheered and whined about being a shopper or stock or whatever. Thunder rumbled.

"Let's do this for Todd Ramos, Employee of the Month," I said and headed to the pharmacy. The first week, when the program started, I'd found some muscle relaxants and some lithium and cumidin and everything else empty, but I still recombed the cabinets, hoping for something else. WalPharm had left a lab coat with B. S. Hert embroidered on the breast and I put that on for Shoppy Days.

"Hey, Miss Thing. What should we do?"

Cathy and DiAngelo stood at the pharmacy counter.

"Oh. Right. First shift. Move Family Planning from Feminine Hygiene to Candy."

"Transfer hanging sign indicator, merchandise and price cards. Inform second shift of store changes," said Cathy.

"Right. Thirty minutes."

"His shoes are not black," said Cathy.

"Yes they are," I said, shaking a bottle and sad to hear nothing rattle inside.

"They have white on them. It says in our manual."

"This is your moment, Cathy. You are First Shift/Cashier. You must be there for the shoppers."

"But it says."

"This is what we will talk about at graduation. You must always be prepared."

Her face closed up and she walked away.

I told DiAngelo. "Life's Services is coming tomorrow. Black shoes and take your hat off. There'll be ladies present. Some respect."

"Respect my ass. I'm not taking this hat off for nobody." He waked away and I shook some more bottles.

All the condoms had gone ages ago. At least people were using them. I had taken Tylenol boxes and written Durex and Life Styles on them.

For several months I'd been struggling with where Family Planning should go and I was tired of it in Feminine Hygiene because most guys are fucking repulsed by the bleeding and everything so then getting the condoms is up to the women and guys associate using them with bloody vaginas so I put Family Planning over with Pain Relief, but who wants to think about safe sex when they've got a headache or just had minor surgery or whatever so I put it back in Feminine Hygiene and now I thought the Candy aisle made tons of sense.

I found myself all fucking caring about this stuff sometimes. This fake WalPharm and the pens should go by the greeting cards and let's move the wrist braces over by the envelopes and then I put on the lab coat and yelled reshelve deodorant between the MoJo Teen-Girl Dolls and the checker boards and got pissed off that, if you thought about it, that made sense, too, and pulled some gum and eye shadow or whatever and locked myself in the Supervisor Room with it and read the labels. I'd memorized the directions and warnings and any active ingredients for seven hundred and forty-six products and had a log going in one of the empty case files.

I'd gotten through most of the cabinets in the pharmacy when I heard screaming. It didn't stop. I drained my travel mug and came out into the store. Cathy and DiAngelo were there next to all the O.B. and Kotex Super Plus with Wings, DiAngelo up on the ladder holding the Family Planning sign and Cathy shook and shouted and clutched her arms around her body.

"What?" I said.

Her lips moved but I couldn't understand what she said, just gasping and sobs so I turned to DiAngelo.

"The chocolate fell out of my pocket."

"Christ. Where is it?"

He lifted his chin towards Cathy.

"Shit. Cathy. Come on. Calm down."

"Yeah," said DiAngelo.

"I gave it to him to put back and he forgot. Come on. You are First Shift."

Cathy did not calm down.

"Graduation, Cathy. Graduation. I want to tell your family how good you were."

"Stop it," she wailed. "Stop about graduation."

"Graduation is awesome, Cathy. You will love it. And your family…"

She stopped shouting, like she just turned off and her body, it was like it shrank and her face became the face of a child, and the change was really dramatic and I stepped toward her and DiAngelo stepped away, higher on the ladder.

"No," said Cathy. "No. My family won't come. I can't live with them anymore. They hurt me."

"Shit," said DiAngelo.

"I want to be a Shopper," said Cathy.

"Yeah. Alright. Alright. Go in back and trade."

After she left, DiAngelo descended. "You don't get to see it. How what you did makes your own people hurt. But it's all the same. I know it when I see it in someone else," he said.

I needed a fucking smoke but when I went to the door the rain came down in buckets.

I went back to the pharmacy that had no medicine.

The program had an excellent placement rate, said Life's All Services. WalPharm was making good on their promise to prioritize the hiring of our graduates but no one had any info on retention or recidivism or anything and it was part of my job to not mention this lack of data. The clients were with me for three months and then poof.

"Second Shift," I yelled.

Because of the clattering with the rain and thunder everyone had to dribble in from the back instead of shoppers making a dramatic entrance from outside and the door ding ding ding. The day was up and running, shoppers weaving through the aisles, stockers inventorying, cashiers ready for cash or check and the shampoo next to the humidifiers and the dishtowels with the crackers and me looking for Todd Ramos's phone number in the telephone book that had slumped against the sliding door when I arrived that morning. I was in love with Todd Ramos. Todd Ramos I want to put your curly blond head between my legs. But you are unlisted.

If it all fell apart when Y2K hit, if everything went under in January, we would be fine, there in WalPharm, us and a bunch of little villages in Zambia or whatever, but those little villages would be fine because they are real and we would be fine because we are fake. The label on a George Foreman Grill says do not touch when hot. Unplug before cleaning.

A few times the thunder made the store sound like it had exploded and the lights flickered.

Keisha came up to the counter with shaving cream, silly putty, a sponge and three Fridgesmart Hot Dog/Deli Keepers rattling around in the red plastic basket hooked on her arm.

"Miss Bianca. There are people in the store."

I thought the first inactive ingredient in Barbasol brand shaving cream was some kind of acid but it could have been water.

"Can I see that canister?" I pointed to her basket.

For sure the contents were under pressure and the can should not be punctured or incinerated.

"There are people, man."

"Yep. Listen. Don't come stoned tomorrow, ok? Life's Services will be here."

"No. People."

A man and a woman, both well-dressed but soggy from the rain, emerged around the calendar display at the end of the center aisle. The woman leaned on the man and walked so it looked like she was in slow motion, her body working real hard but not getting anywhere. About ten trainees, some in their WalPharm shirts, some with baskets and DiAngelo in his purple suit followed along behind.

The man darted out in front of the woman when he saw me behind the counter, his eyes focused on the lab coat.

"Shit," I said. "Do you come in peace?"

"My wife is in labor and we got lost and the car. The rain. Please."

"Oh no. No."

"What a godsend. A WalPharm out here."

"No. No."

The wife groaned a little and clenched her jaw.

"No. This isn't true. They just left the sign up."

"Call an ambulance," said DiAngelo.

"Is there a chair?" said the woman.

All eighteen trainees had gathered.

"Better get that lady some dry clothes," said Roy.

"Yeah, yeah," I said.

There was a bunch of pandemonium with Keisha with her cellular phone, flip, flipping it, I just can't get any signal and people tore around pulling clothing and Cathy shouted about how this is Shoppy Day and we only have an hour to finish all the lists and someone said that Roy knows about cars because Roy told us all the time about the sweet ride he was going to buy when he started earning and Roy said I'm not going out in that mess to get electrocuted then we were all in the Teaching Room with the man and the woman except Keisha who yelled from the Supervisor Room that the phone was down.

Everyone sat in their chairs like we were going to watch a movie.

The man looked at me.

"Would you like some Tylenol or an antacid?" I asked.

"I guess I could use an antacid. Yeah."

I scooted out quick because they freaked me out with how pale he looked and her groaning and took a long time comparing labels on the generic and brand-name products, even though I knew everything they said and even though they were all expired.

On the way back into the room I shouted to Keisha.

"Nothing," she said.

All the trainees had not moved and the man ran his hand through his hair and swept his eyes over the crowd as if waiting for someone to make a sudden move he'd have to defend against. The woman gripped onto the sides of her seat.

"Oh good," he said. "Honey, the pharmacist is back."

"Get these people out of here," she said.

"Would you mind?" he said to me.

"I need to lie down," she said.

I really liked this woman. I liked how everything she said was straightforward and doable.

"Alright, guys. Go. Go finish your lists. Finish Shoppy Day," I said. I looked at the woman and the hard floor. "Les and Cathy get those drop cloths out of storage."

Cathy came back with a stack of cloths and she looked very worried.

"Don't worry," I told her. I was very worried.

She buried her head in the cloths and then handed them to me.

"Always be prepared," she said.

"Right. Right." I shut the door behind her.

The woman said, "This is happening. Squat. I want to squat."

"Shit. No. Wait. We need an ambulance," I said.

"Squat," said the woman.

"What should I do?" the husband asked me.

"Shit. The pants," I said.

I was shaking and had to pee and I was buzzed from the travel mug and I wrapped the softest drop cloth around the woman's hips and tucked it up over her belly and her belly was so tight and touching this woman

I didn't know and she leaned on me and her husband and we sank down together. The woman breathed and stared at nothing but she was quiet, only her breath hissing and panting and a constant hum coming out of her that I couldn't hear I could just feel it. She sort of fell back against her husband and he leaned against the wall so he cradled her in his arms and between his legs and I held onto her hips. I wasn't sure why I had her hips but I did and I could feel all the muscles tightening and tightening. And this thing I had wanted came up in me kind of like a mist. I remembered how I'd wanted to be a veterinarian when I was little and I wrapped tape around this gerbil's leg and I'd read all these books about a guy in England who worked with cows and dogs and sheep. I remembered this guy out in the cold barns and he'd strip off and soap up and shove his arms deep in a cow to help it get the baby out.

I ran my hand over the embroidery on my lab coat. B. S. Hert.

I looked up at Todd Ramos. I wanted to make him proud, Employee of the Month, Todd Ramos.

I opened the door and everyone was standing out in the hall.

"Into the store, you guys. Someone go to First Aid and get all the alcohol and swabs and then those dish towels."

I got the man to put on a dry shirt and got her in a dry shirt and her pants off under the drop cloth and he held her and counted breaths. DiAngelo came in. He opened the door and came right in with shopping baskets full of stuff and knelt down by the woman.

"Hello, Mama," he said, his voice real soft and gentle like it was all over and the kid was out and the woman wasn't panting and staring into the distance.

She glanced at him and grabbed his hand and her husband's and groaned into the next contraction. DiAngelo pet the back of her hand.

"Y'all doing real good."

He tried to stand up but the woman did not let go of him.

"Now," she said.

Keisha shouted, "I got through."

"It is happening," I yelled.

I dumped alcohol all over my hands and spread out the towels and the contractions didn't stop and everything happened fast and the backs of her thighs so white and it smelled of blood and shit and Keisha hollering directions through the wall, push down, guide the head and when the baby came out it was blue and red and covered in creamy stuff and it screamed and then a big answering yell came through the walls from everyone in the store.

DiAngelo held up the woman and the husband came around and the two of us wrapped the baby in a sweat shirt and the cord still coming out of his belly down into his mother's vagina and handed their child up into her reaching arms.

She smiled this tiny smile that only made it as far as the baby, just for him, and he quieted. Then she turned so the smile made it to the man.

"It's a boy."

The man and the woman held the baby against her chest and I sat back on the ground and DiAngelo stood up.

"Well," he said. "That sure was nice."

The man looked up and searched in his face and said, "We're going to name him DiAngelo."

The ambulance arrived and the medics bundled the woman and the baby and hauled them up into the big square back of the vehicle.

"Now hang on a second," DiAngelo said and touched the man's arm before he went out the door. The man paused but glanced at his wife rolling out through the rain.

"Here. Here's something for your little man."

DiAngelo took off his black hat with the silver band and handed it, right side up, to the husband. The door whooshed shut and the man and the woman and the baby and the ambulance all drove away and the clouds and the rain and the gray streets swallowed the whole deal.

DiAngelo's hair was permed out straight and combed back and creased where the hat had been. Splotches of pale and hairless skin shone out through the groomed strands.

He turned to us and ran his hand over his head a few times.

"Looking sharp, DiAngelo," said Keisha. "You looking sharp."

He flashed his teeth and rocked back on his heals, "Ah, well, you shoulda seen Miss Thing in there. Caught that baby right out of its mama."

Out of the blue Cathy shouted, "Elvira did it."

Cathy's face was all screwed up in panic and fear and she pointed to the checkout counter. There was a bag of pretzels and some red drink in Dixie Cups.

"Elvira did it."

"Oh, Cathy," I said. I looked down at my lab coat with blood on the sleeves. "That's ok."

Her expression did not change.

"That was a good rule to break," said DiAngelo. "When I leave here and get a job, that's the kind of rule I'm going to break. I'm going to know when to celebrate."

I said, "Let's have a big old party and open up all the red drink and the purple drink. Let's have a big party, just us."

Les coaxed Cathy into drinking a cup of red drink and we all downed shots till our lips turned bubble gum red and Cathy giggled at her reflection in the sunglasses display mirror and DiAngelo told about the woman grabbing his hand and Keisha told how the phone lines came up and I thought about that baby's head stuck out of its mother. Like an alien. Crushed and blue. But I still felt, in spots in my neck and head and stomach, that this baby and this mother and father were true and then the cigar in DiAngelo's pocket peeked up and Cathy saw it and she raised up her arm and pointed.

"Cigar," she said.

"Shit," I said.

"Cigar," she said again.

She turned in a circle, arms out, smiling to the ceiling.

"Cigars for everyone," she said, "It's a baby. Baby DiAngelo."

ACKNOWLEDGMENTS

This is where writers get to break down the great myth of *Writer As Lone Artist*. Wonderful. It is impossible to name all the people who have had a hand in these stories, there is not enough space for all the librarians and teachers I have known, for all the writers whose work has contributed to my own, but I'll attempt to name here people who have inspired and offered talent and knowledge to these stories. Andy Nicholson, Jonathan Seyfried, Eva Raison, Dr. Davis, Aurora Brackett, G.G. Simmons, Jes, João Costa and faculty and workshop-mates at UNLV. Thanks also to Ashley Siebels for her eye and heart and hours. This book is in your hands because of everyone at Jackleg Press who opened their arms to the manuscript, especially Jennifer Harris and Juan Martinez. And, of course, thank you to my family.

VERSIONS OF THESE PIECES HAVE APPEARED IN THE FOLLOWING PUBLICATIONS:

"To Receive My Services You Must Be Dying and Alone," Indiana Review

"Holy Palmer," The Adirondack Review

"Chalk Walker," (originally titled "Downlands,") Specks

"Everything We Learn We Learn Again," McNeese Review

"The Printed Baby," Quiddity

"And with Such Great Effort to Achieve," The Manchester Review

"Sex Ed," Jet Fuel Review

V. Joshua Adams, Scott Shibuya Brown, Brian Rivka Clifton, Brittney Corrigan, Jessica Cuello, Barbara Cully, Alison Cundiff, Neil de la Flor, Genevieve DeGuzman, Suzanne Frischkorn, Victoria Garza, Reginald Gibbons, Joachim Glage, Caroline Goodwin, Kathryn Kruse, Meagan Lehr, Brigitte Lewis, Jenny Magnus, D.K. McCutchen, Jean McGarry, Rita Mookerjee, Mamie Morgan, Alexis Orgera, Karen Rigby, Jo Salas, Maureen Seaton, Kristine Snodgrass, Cornelia Maude Spelman, Peter Stenson, Melissa Studdard, Curious Theatre, Gemini Wahhaj, Megan Weiler, David Welch, Cassandra Whitaker, David Wesley Williams

jacklegpress.org